Favorite Scary Stories of American Children

"Children who like Alvin Schwartz's
Favorite Scary Stories to Tell in the Dark
will be thrilled with this collection."
—**Booklist**

"A wonderful collection of much-loved tales."
—**Ruth Rowan, Lakeland (FL) Ledger**

"These stories have stood the test of time
through retelling, and they are identified
by children across the nation to be
among their favorites."
—**Sandy Donnan, Orlando Sentinel**

"Excellent"
—The Washington Times

"[This] book will serve its purpose well...
for classrooms, storytelling settings,
sleepovers, and read-aloud sessions."
—**Molly Kinney, School Library Journal**

FOR OTHER BOOKS APPROPRIATE FOR YOUNG READERS
AND FOR STORYTELLING, SEE THE LIST ON PAGE 127

SYMBOLS

For children age 5 or 6.
For reading or telling to a child in your lap.

For children age 7 or 8.
For reading or telling to children in a group.

For children age 9 or 10.
For reading or telling to the child,
or for the child to read alone.

The age-rating of stories has to do with how their content—the themes, conflicts, and "fearfulness"—matches with the emotional development of children. While some older children will enjoy the stories for younger ones, others may find them "babyish." The vocabulary of all stories is appropriate to nine- or ten-year-olds reading on their own.

FAVORITE
SCARY STORIES
OF AMERICAN CHILDREN

Richard and Judy Dockrey Young

August House Publishers, Inc.

LITTLE ROCK

Published 1990, 1999 by August House, Inc,
P.O. Box 3223, Little Rock, Arkansas 72203,
501-372-5450.

Printed in the United States of America

10 9 8 7 6 5 4 3

LIBRARY OF CONGRESS CATALOGING-IN-PUBLICATION DATA
Favorite scary stories of American children / [edited by]
Richard and Judy Dockrey Young. — 1st reillustrated ed.
p. cm.
Summary: A collection, selected by children as their favorites, of
twenty-three spooky tales from a variety of ethnic traditions.
ISBN 0-87483-563-1
1. Horror tales. [1. Horror stories. 2. Folklore.]
I. Young, Richard, 1946–   . II. Young, Judy Dockrey, 1949–   .
PZ8.1.F238   1999
398.2'0973'07—dc21   99-28780
CIP

Project editor and book design: Joy Freeman
Cover art and book illustration: Don Bell

The paper used in this publication meets the minimum
requirements of the American National Standard for
Information Sciences—Permanence of Paper for
Printed Library Materials, ANSI Z39.48-1984

AUGUST HOUSE, INC.   PUBLISHERS   LITTLE ROCK

For Teresa, Tom, Nicole, and Claire

CONTENTS

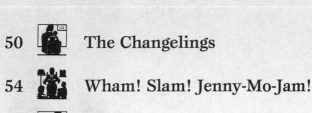

INTRODUCTION

We are professional storytellers based at Silver Dollar City, Missouri, who learn and retell tales from the vast American oral tradition. The stories most requested by children, especially in autumn and especially at nighttime performances, are scary stories. We have chosen for this new collection of scary stories the ones that children most often tell to us, most often ask to hear, or most often identify as their favorites.

For a story to become a favorite among children, it must have been told for many years, sometimes even many generations. As a result, some of the tales in this collection have been published in previous anthologies around the turn of the century. Alongside these old chestnuts are folktales in variants that have never until now been in print. We have also included several scary stories from Southeast Asia that have been brought to America and told as favorites here in the post-Vietnam era.

Children love scary stories and, in fact, benefit from them by facing and mastering the little moments of "fear for fun" these tales provide.

Naturally, every storyteller needs to know the audience and judge the appropriateness of every frightening folktale. We recommend that before you read or present these stories to the children in your care, you read and consider the information in the Afterword to this collection. We hope you and all the children who read or hear these stories will find as much pleasure in them as we and the children who gave them to us have. We've enjoyed them, and we've enjoyed bringing them to you.

Richard Alan Young
Judy Dockrey Young
Harrison, Arkansas
May 1990

OLD RAW HEAD

Deep in the wooded hills and hollows of the Ozark Mountains there lived an old conjuring woman who knew all the herbs and cures and roots and magic spells. She had one friend: a lean, mean wild razorback hog came by her cabin to eat her kitchen garbage. Some folks say he ate so many of her roots and magic potions that he could walk and talk like a man. Some folks say.

Every October the hill people slaughter hogs and put up the meat into a smokehouse for the long winter. When the wind blows cold and the frost comes and the leaves turn, it's hog-scalding time. Men gather from miles around and drive hogs into rail-fence pens. The animals are slaughtered and the carcasses scalded enough to get the bristle hair off. Then the butchering begins: by sundown, the meat is all packed to go home, and the raw skinned hogs' heads and the bloody bones are all that's left out of the burlap sacks.

One lazy hillbilly stole hogs from his neighbors at hog-scalding time, and he must have rounded up that conjuring woman's pet, too. After the butchering

that day, he rode away with a bag of meat and a skinned head in his wagon, but the wagon wheel hit a bump and out onto the dark road rolled the old raw head.

"Bloody bones," said Old Raw Head, "get up and dance!"

The bloody bones back at the butchering pens jumped up and danced around, and pulled together again, and came and got the head!

Old Raw Head ran into the woods, and went to all the critters and borrowed things to wear. He borrowed the panther's fangs; he borrowed the bear's claws; he borrowed the raccoon's tail. And he went to the lazy hillbilly's house.

The old man and the old woman were in bed when they heard a scrabbling, clattering sound, and sparks jumped off the coals in the fireplace. The old man got up to see what was the matter. He looked and looked and looked and couldn't find the intruder. Then he looked up the chimney.

"Land o' Goshen," said the old man, "what've you got those big old eyes for?"

"To see your grave," said a deep, hollow voice up the chimney.

The old man ran away.

A minute later he came back and looked up the chimney again. "Land o' Goshen," he said, "what've you got those great big claws for?"

"To dig your grave," said the deep, dark voice.

The old man ran away again.

A few minutes later he came back and looked up the chimney again. "Land o' Goshen," he said, "what've you got that big bushy tail for?"

"To sweep your grave," said the rumbling, rolling voice.

The old man ran and hid under the bed and said, "Land O' Goshen, what've you got those long sharp teeth for?"

"TO EAT YOU UP," said Old Raw Head, and he came down the chimney and carried off the lazy old thief and stole his horse!

No one ever saw the old man again, but they saw Old Raw Head, wearing the old man's shirt and overalls, riding that stolen horse and carrying his raw skinned head up high against the full moon.

And every Hallowe'en, if the moon is full, they see Old Raw Head with his eyes glowing like hot coals, riding through the hills and hollows, deep in the Ozark Mountains. And if you go there, you can see him, too.

Skunnee Wundee and the Stone Giant

When people and animals were still able to talk to one another, an Indian boy named Skunnee Wundee went out for a walk in the woods. His mother had told him never to go up the river to the place where the Stone Giants lived, but the boy was so busy skipping rocks across the river he forgot. Pretty soon, there he was, right in the middle of the circle of stones where the Stone Giants lived.

He turned to run downriver to the place where people lived, but he ran right into the feet of a Stone Giant. The giant was as tall as a pine tree. The giant picked Skunnee Wundee up and said:

"You're a people! I eat peoples!"

"Oh, no," cried Skunnee Wundee, "Don't eat me!"

The Stone Giant thought about it for a while. Stone Giants are not very smart. "Why not?" the giant asked at last.

"Because," said Skunnee Wundee, "I can skip a rock further across the river than you can."

The giant had to think about that for quite a while. "I'll eat you anyway," said the Stone Giant.

"No, wait!" yelled Skunnee Wundee. "Let me

prove to you how well I can skip a rock."

The Stone Giant put the boy down and picked up a boulder as big as an Indian family's lodge. "I got my stone," said the giant. "You pick yours."

Skunnee Wundee looked all around the rocks by the river, trying to find a good flat one to skip across the water. He heard a little voice say, "Choose me, Skunnee Wundee, choose me!"

There on the riverbank was a little turtle, just about the size of a good flat rock. Skunnee Wundee picked up the turtle. The turtle pulled its head and feet into its shell, and tried to look as much like a rock as possible. But the stupid Stone Giant was very easy to fool.

The giant threw his great big rock, and it skipped ten times along the water before it sank into the deep river. "Ten times," said the Stone Giant. "I win."

"Not yet, you don't," said Skunnee Wundee, and he threw the little turtle into the river. The turtle skipped just like a flat rock, two, three, four, five

times.
Then
the turtle
put out its feet
and began to kick.
Six times the turtle
skipped, seven, eight, nine,
ten. Then the turtle began to swim. Eleven, twelve, thirteen times, the swimming turtle looked like a skipping rock. Fourteen, fifteen, sixteen times! The turtle swam all the way to the other side and sat on the other riverbank looking like a rock.

"I win," said Skunnee Wundee.

The Stone Giant was so mad that he shook and shook, and shook himself into a thousand pieces. All the pieces fell into a big rock pile.

Skunnee Wundee crossed the river, thanked the turtle, and went home. Don't ask how he crossed the river. That's a different story!

The Golem

The old folks say there is a statue in a park in New York City of a big, ugly man with his hand up near his ear. Every day, pigeons perch on the statue, and children come by and wonder why such an ugly statue is there. And this is why:

Years and years ago, a wealthy rabbi came to America with his family. They came from the Old Country and brought with them many wooden crates of household goods. One especially heavy crate was put in the basement unopened. Years passed.

The rabbi grew old and taught his son to be a rabbi. The old man died and his son took his place after graduating from school. The son who was a rabbi grew old, but he never married and had no children. So he took in a young apprentice who wanted to study to become a rabbi some day.

The old rabbi died quietly one day, and when the young apprentice was cleaning out the basement, he opened the wooden crate for the first time in years. Inside was an ugly man carved out of white stone. He was a golem! He was a creature cut from

stone and brought to life to work for his master. No wonder the first rabbi's family had been wealthy!

The young apprentice looked inside the lid of the crate, and there was a small roll of paper. On it was written the True Name of God, a word so powerful that very few men or women knew it. The young apprentice put the roll of paper with the Name on it into the golem's left ear.

The golem blinked his stone eyelids and stepped out of the crate.

"Yes, Master," growled the golem in a voice like far-away thunder.

"Clean up the basement!" said the apprentice.

The golem went to work and the apprentice went upstairs to make some tea. Suddenly the golem came stomping up the stairs.

"I am finished, Master," said the golem. "Give me something else to do."

The apprentice looked down into the basement and saw that it was all cleaned up. "Clean up the house," said the apprentice. The golem went to work, and the young man sat down to drink his tea. Before the tea was cool enough to drink, the golem stomped back into the kitchen.

"I am finished, Master," snarled the golem. "Give me something else to do!"

The apprentice looked and saw that the entire house was clean.

"Mow the yard and trim the hedge and prune the trees," said the young man. The golem went to work, and the apprentice sat down to read the evening newspaper. Before he even finished the headlines, the golem kicked the door open and came in.

"I am finished, Master!" growled the golem. "Give me something else to do!"

The apprentice tried to take the roll of paper out of the golem's ear, to turn it back into stone. The golem wouldn't let him.

"I like being alive," howled the golem, picking the young man up and shaking him like a rag doll. "Give me something else to do!"

"Paint the house and fix the fence and water the flowers and sweep the sidewalk and wash the windows!" yelled the apprentice. The golem went to work, and the young man ran down the street to another retired rabbi's house.

When the kind old rabbi let the young man in, the apprentice told what had happened. "You have done a very foolish thing," said the old rabbi. "You should never play with things you do not understand."

Just at that moment, the golem knocked the door off its hinges and stomped into the old rabbi's house. The apprentice tried again to take the roll of paper out of the golem's ear, but the stone creature wouldn't let him. The golem picked up the apprentice and began banging the young man's head against the ceiling.

"I like being alive," screamed the golem. "Now, give me *something else to DO!*"

"Golem," said the old rabbi in a soft voice.

The golem stopped banging the apprentice against the ceiling.

"Yes, Rabbi," said the stone thing.

"Put the young man down," said the rabbi. "My seven grandchildren are playing in the park just down the street. Go there and answer all their questions."

The stone thing dropped the apprentice and stomped down the street to the park. It sat down and started answering all the children's questions.

"Why is the sky blue?" asked a little girl.

"What are stars made of?" asked a little boy.

"Why don't cats like dogs?" asked a pair of twins.

An hour and seven thousand answers later, the golem reached slowly up to his ear, pulled out the roll of paper, and turned back into stone. And he's still sitting there today.

Ghost Of Vengeance

From the Great City with its temples and palaces, from the district called Yotsuya, came a samurai swordsman who took himself a beautiful wife named Oiwa. She called him only Otto-san, saying politely, "My Husband." At first the two were very happy together, but with time the restless warrior's affections began to wander. At a great banquet Otto-san saw the lovely young maiden Matsue, and fell as much in love with her as he had once been with Oiwa.

The path away from the banquet that moonless night led along a cliff above the sea, and, wanting to free himself to marry Matsue, the samurai pretended to stumble in the darkness and shoved his attentive wife over the edge.

At dawn the samurai and his friends combed the beach below the cliff and found the broken body of Oiwa, whose death he had told them was an accident.

After the funeral, the warrior was sleeping on his mat in the empty house, glad about his new-found freedom, when the wind outside moaned in the trees, and the sliding paper walls of the sleeping room shook. Slowly, in the moonlight, one wall-door slid open. There stood the ghost of Oiwa.

Her long hair, so neatly combed and arranged in life, hung loose about her shoulders; her lovely kimono was gone, and she wore a long, flowing white robe. Her face, once beautiful, was ugly and dirty. Some of her teeth were missing, and one eye lay over to the side. Her arms were bony, like those

of an old woman, and her hands were like claws.

She said one word: "Vengeance."

Otto-san screamed and fled from the house.

The next night he slept in an abandoned house nearby, hoping to escape the sight of his dead wife. The single paper lantern he used for light hung above his mat. At midnight he awoke. The room

seemed empty, with only the paper lantern and ivy vines growing in through a break in the wall. Slowly, as the candle in the lantern began to flicker out, the samurai thought he saw his wife's face in the designs on the paper. Slowly, the vines below the lantern began to crawl like snakes into the shape of Oiwa's body. The wind blew in through a crack and swung the lantern. The candle inside tipped over, and the paper began to burn. Oiwa's face was clear in the lantern. The vines reached up toward the warrior. The bottom of the burning lantern flapped like a jaw talking; two burning eyes looked at the husband.

"Vengeance," said the lantern.

The man leaped off his sleeping mat, drew his sword, cut his way out through the bamboo wall, and ran screaming down the path away from the house.

Other warriors, friends of Otto-san, began to see Oiwa, too. Two men were drinking tea and she came to them asking for revenge. The next time they saw the murderer, they drew their swords and tried to kill him, so strong was Oiwa's spell over them. The husband shouted his friends' names. "Gunze," he called out, "Kaminasu, what are you doing this for?"

"Vengeance," said their mouths, but it was Oiwa's voice that he heard. The ghost of his wife appeared beside the fighting men. Otto-san fled, but while Oiwa's body stayed where it stood, her neck grew very long and her head followed him down the path. He swung his sword and cut off her head, but it just dropped to the ground like a melon and laughed at him.

The next time he saw his friends they did not remember what had happened.

One day Otto-san persuaded Matsue to come to his house to see how finely she would live once they were married. While she was looking at the home, she heard a woman's voice talking to the warrior in another room. She hid behind a paper screen to listen to the conversation. All she heard was a woman's voice, and how Otto-san trembled with fear. She thought he was afraid of being caught with that other woman—Matsue did not know the woman was Oiwa. The ghost floated along the floor, with a long, long tail of white drifting behind and its mutilated face restored to its former beauty. As if they were young lovers again, the ghost whispered in the warrior's ear.

"Vengeance," she said.

Matsue no longer trusted Otto-san and became enraged with jealousy.

At last by much persuading, the warrior convinced Matsue to marry him. A great engagement party was prepared. All their friends and relatives came. Oiwa came, too.

The ghost came into the party room and stood against the wall. Her face was as horrible as ever, with broken teeth and drooping eyeballs, her wild hair mixed with seaweed swirled about even though there was no wind. At first Otto-san tried to distract everyone from looking at the ghost by boasting and talking loudly. He did not know that no one else could see her. The ghost grew larger.

Otto-san tried to hide back against the opposite wall, knocking over a table and teacups, trying to escape the huge head that slowly filled the room. In desperation he drew his sword and swung it all about, trying to cut through the ghostly face that overpowered him. All his friends stared and muttered to each other. Matsue blushed and left, never to return to this madman. All his friends laughed at what he did and left in disgust. Oiwa laughed, too, but no one heard her.

The moon was dark again, and the path along the cliffs was as windy as before. A gentle woman in life, the mutilated body of Oiwa walked beside her husband, her flesh hanging loose off her skeletal face. It was too late for regret, too late for repentance. It was time for insanity and death.

"Vengeance," said the skull with the long, black hair.

The samurai stepped off the cliff and was gone.

Oiwa was gone, too.

But on windy nights, when the paper lanterns blow, and the candle falls, and the lantern begins to burn, if you dare to look closely enough, you will see the face of Oiwa, the Ghost of Vengeance!

The Hobbyahs

Once there were an old man, an old woman, and a little girl, who all lived together in a little house made of hempstalks. The old man had a little dog named Terpy. One night the hungry ugly Hobbyahs came and stomped around the little hempstalk house chanting:

> *Hobbyahs! Hobbyahs! Hobbyahs!*
> *Tear down the hempstalks!*
> *Eat the old man and woman!*
> *Carry off the little girl!*

But little dog Terpy barked so loud that the Hobbyahs all ran away. The old man turned in his bed and said, "Little Dog Terpy barks so that I can neither slumber nor sleep. If I live until the morning, I will cut off his tail!" And in the morning, the old man cut off the little dog's tail.

The next night the Hobbyahs came again, and circled the little hempstalk house saying:

> *Hobbyahs! Hobbyahs! Hobbyahs!*
> *Tear down the hempstalks!*

Eat the old man and woman!
Carry off the little girl!

But little dog Terpy barked out loud and the Hobbyahs all ran away. The old man stirred in his sleep and said, "Little Dog Terpy barks so that I can neither slumber nor sleep. If I live until the morning, I will cut off one of his legs." And the next day, he did!

The very next night the hungry ugly Hobbyahs returned to the little house and danced around it calling:

Hobbyahs! Hobbyahs! Hobbyahs!
Tear down the hempstalks!
Eat the old man and woman!
Carry off the little girl!

Once again Terpy barked and scared the Hobbyahs, who all ran away. But the old man turned over in his bed and growled, "Little Dog Terpy barks so that I can neither slumber nor sleep. If I live until the morning, I will cut off another of his legs!" So, in the morning the old man cut off another of the little dog's legs.

By night the Hobbyahs came again, and said:

Hobbyahs! Hobbyahs! Hobbyahs!
Tear down the hempstalks!
Eat the old man and woman!
Carry off the little girl!

But little dog Terpy barked so that the Hobbyahs all ran off; and the old man said, "Little Dog Terpy barks so that I can neither slumber nor sleep. If I live until the morning, I will cut off another one of his legs!" And the next morning, that's what he did.

The next night the hungry ugly Hobbyahs came again, and hopped about the hempstalk house hollering:

Hobbyahs! Hobbyahs! Hobbyahs!
Tear down the hempstalks!
Eat the old man and woman!
Carry off the little girl!

Terpy barked again. The Hobbyahs heard him and all ran away. But the old man tossed in his bed and said, "Little Dog Terpy barks so that I can neither slumber nor sleep. If I live until the morning, I will cut off his leg!" And the next morning, he did.

When the sun went down and the moon came up the Hobbyahs came again:

Hobbyahs! Hobbyahs! Hobbyahs!
Tear down the hempstalks!
Eat the old man and woman!
Carry off the little girl!

But little dog Terpy barked, and all the Hobbyahs ran away. The old man rolled over in his bed and said, "Little Dog Terpy barks so that I can neither slumber nor sleep. If I live until the morning, I will cut off his head." And when the sun came up, he did.

The Hobbyahs came back to the little house that night. They danced around it and sang:

Hobbyahs! Hobbyahs! Hobbyahs!
Tear down the hempstalks!
Eat the old man and woman!
Carry off the little girl!

Nobody barked. And the Hobbyahs tore down the hempstalk house, ate the old man and woman, and carried the little girl off in a big burlap bag. And they went to their den and hung up the bag with the little girl in it. And they opened the bag, and poked their hungry ugly heads into the bag and said:

Look at meeeeee!

And the little girl cried. The Hobbyahs went to sleep, because Hobbyahs sleep in the daytime.

The little girl didn't go to sleep—she cried. And a hunter with a big black dog came by and heard her crying. When he looked in the bag and asked her why she was crying, she told him. He put his big black dog in the bag and took the little girl to his home.

The next night the Hobbyahs opened the bag and said:

Look at meeeeee!

And the big black dog jumped out of the bag and ate all the Hobbyahs up.

And there are no Hobbyahs now.

RAP...RAP...RAP!

Shylock Bones was the greatest ghost detective of them all. There wasn't ever a mystery about a ghost that he couldn't solve—including this one. One fine day a lady came into Shylock Bones's office and said, "Help me, Mr. Bones, I am afraid my house is haunted."

Shylock Bones got out his big plaid hat and his big rubber boots and his big magnifying glass that made things look bigger, and off they went to the lady's house in the spookiest part of town. They went inside, and the lady said, "Listen!"

Shylock Bones listened. He heard something very far away in the big old house going, "Rap... rap...rap!" Shylock frowned and said, "It may be a ghost, Ma'am. Never fear, my dear, Shylock Bones is here." And he went to work.

Shylock Bones searched the basement. "Rap ... rap ... rap!" he heard in the distance. He searched the first floor. "Rap...rap...rap!" It was a little louder. He went upstairs.

"Rap...rap...rap!" He searched all the bedrooms and looked under all the beds. He searched

the bathroom and tried to look under the bathtub. He searched all the closets and looked inside all the shoes.

"Rap...rap...rap!" It sounded a little bit louder. He searched all the drawers and shook out all the pajamas and looked inside the toy chest. Then he turned to the lady, who had been following him. "Let's search the attic," he said.

They went out in the hall. They heard, "Rap…rap…rap!" It sounded louder than downstairs. The lady pulled on a rope and the ladder to the attic came down from the ceiling.

"Rap…rap…rap!" It was definitely louder. They climbed up into the attic. Shylock got out his flashlight and his magnifying glass. He looked through his magnifying glass. Everything looked bigger, but that didn't help any.

"Rap…rap…rap!" It sounded nearby. They started searching the attic. They searched in the trunks and they searched in the old boxes. They searched in the old birdcage and they searched in the pickle barrel. Shylock Bones didn't ask why there was a pickle barrel in her attic.

"Rap…rap…rap!" They were getting closer.

Shylock shined his flashlight on an old chest-of-drawers.

"Rap…Rap…Rap!" He opened the top drawer. Nothing.

"Rap…Rap…RAP!" He opened the second drawer. Nothing!

*"Rap…RAP…**RAP!**"* He opened the third drawer. Still nothing!

"RAP…RAP…RAP!" He opened the bottom drawer. And there it was!

A sheet of WRAPPING PAPER!

Stop The Coffin!

Once upon a time, a long time ago, there was a country boy who went to town to see the sights. He didn't have much money, so he couldn't stay in a hotel. He decided to sleep where no one would bother him: he went to sleep in the cemetery.

In the middle of the night, he woke up when something bumped him on the foot. He looked up, and there was a shiny rosewood coffin. He got up and moved. The coffin moved, too. He moved a little further. The coffin moved a little further. He got up and started to run. The coffin floated up into the air and started to follow him.

He ran out the gate of the graveyard. The coffin followed him. He ran across the flowerbed, trampling the flowers. The coffin came, too. He ran through the poultry yard and scared all the chickens. The coffin scared them, too.

He ran through the park and knocked over a picnic table. The coffin knocked one over, too. He ran through the stable and scared all the horses. The coffin scared the horses, too.

He ran through the grocery store and pushed over

the cracker barrel. The coffin pushed one over, too.

He jumped through the back window and broke the window out. The coffin broke a window out, too.

He ran into the drug store and there it all ended.

He opened a box and ate some cough drops… and stopped the coughin'.

RAGGELUG

Once there was a little-bitty bunny rabbit named Raggelugg who lived with his mother Molly Cottontail in a nest in the middle of the big meadow. Every single morning since the day Raggelugg was born, his mother would hop up and hop out of the nest and say, "Raggelugg, I've got to get me something to eat and a drink of water. While I'm gone, you sit right here and don't you move!"

Every single day he'd sit right there and wouldn't move.

This went on for many days. She'd hop up and hop out of the nest and say, "Raggelugg, I've got to get me something to eat and a drink of water. While I'm gone, you sit right here and don't you move!" Now Raggelugg had had an awful lot of sit-right-here-and-don't-you-move lessons, and he was good at it. He would sit there in the nest, and he wouldn't move his nose and he wouldn't move his toes, and he wouldn't move anything at all, except sometimes he'd put up one long, white ear to hear if his mother was coming back.

One pretty day the sun was shining and the sky

was blue; the clouds were going across in the breeze, and Raggelugg found out that if he just raised one little rabbit eyebrow, he could see what was going on in the sky. And if he put up one long ear, he could hear what was going on in the meadow.

Then, he would put up the other ear to hear what was going on.

Well, this day, he put up one ear, and he heard *rustle ... rustle ... rustle.* And he put up the other ear

and heard *rustle...rustle...rustle.*

Raggelugg said to himself, "I wonder what that is. It sounds like the breeze, but it's too loud." So he put up both ears, and he heard *whish...whish... whish.* And he said to himself, "I wonder what that is. It sounds like something moving in the meadow grass, but I don't hear any feet walking." So he put both ears up really far, and listened so hard he got wrinkles between his ears. And he heard *rattle... rattle...rustle...rustle...whish...whish.*

And he said to himself, "I wonder what that is. I'm going to sit up on my hind feet and look out of the nest and see what that is. I'm a big bunny now. Momma told me not to move, but I'm three full weeks old now. I'm going to sit up and see what that is."

And he sat up.

And he saw what it was.

It was a great big, black snake that looked him straight in the eyes and said, "Hissssss!"

The snake made a grab at Raggelugg, but Raggelugg dodged. The hungry snake missed Raggelugg's head, but he caught him by the ear. Raggelugg was terribly afraid, and he started fighting and hopping and yelling, "MOMMA!"

Slowly, the hungry snake wrapped himself around Raggelugg and began to squeeze. And Raggelugg yelled *"Momma!"* not quite as loud as before. And the hungry snake wrapped even tighter around Raggelugg, and Raggelugg said, "...momma..." But she'd heard him the first time.

Here came Molly Cottontail across the meadow,

hopping as fast as she could hop. She saw the snake and jumped into the air and kicked the snake with her hind foot. She was terribly scared, but she had to do what she had to do. The snake said, "Hissss!" but he didn't let go of Raggelugg.

Molly hopped in front of the snake and turned her tail and kicked the snake in the head with both her hind feet. The snake let go of Raggelugg...and grabbed Raggelugg's momma!

But Molly said, "Run, Raggelugg, run!" and she pulled loose from the snake so he had nothing but a mouthful of bunny fur. Then she put up her white tail, a sign for Raggelugg to follow her, and she ran and she ran, and Raggelugg followed and he followed. And she ran and she ran, and Raggelugg followed and he followed.

They ran all the way across the meadow faster than the snake could ever follow, and she made them a new nest under a gooseberry bush. And they sat up close to each other and wiggled their noses until they were sure the snake had gone on his way and wouldn't bother them any more.

After a while, Molly Cottontail looked over at Raggelugg, who now had one ear that hung over funny to one side, and said, "Raggelugg, I've still got to get me something to eat and a drink of water. While I'm gone you sit...right...here and don't... you...move."

And this time Raggelugg sat right there, and he didn't move.

She's Got Me!

Once, not long ago, in the farmland in the North, there was a community of plain folks who used the old-style farm tools instead of modern tractors and things. The menfolk were out in the field working one day, and two young girls had taken supper out to their fathers and uncles and brothers in the field. Walking home with nothing left of the meal except the dirty forks in their apron pockets, the girls passed the old iron gate of the graveyard.

"There's where they buried that old witch today," said the sassy girl to the polite girl just as the sun was going down.

"Oh, you must not speak ill of the dead," said the polite girl. "That isn't nice at all!"

"I'm not afraid of that old woman," said the mean girl. "You're just a fraidy-cat. Why, I'd go in and just spit on that old woman's grave. But you'd be too scared to come with me!"

"Even if she were a witch," said the polite girl, "it would be wrong of you to do that. Besides, you'd just go in there and wait behind a tree. Then you'd come out and claim you'd done it!"

"I would not," the other answered. "I'll just go right in and spit on that old witch's grave. And to prove I did it…" she pulled a fork out of her apron pocket as she spoke. "I'll stick this fork into the grave to prove I was there. You can go in tomorrow in broad daylight and see."

With the fork in her hand, the sassy girl went through the old iron gate into the dark graveyard and walked among the trees and tombstones until

she came to the fresh grave of the old woman. The sun was down, and long shadows fell across the pile of dirt that covered the grave. It was hard to see in the darkness, but the brazen girl leaned over and spit on the dirt.

"Take that, old witch," said the mean girl, and she bent over and stuck the fork into the dirt to show she had been there. Just then, she felt something grab onto the hem of her long dress. When she tried to stand up, it pulled at her dress. She looked down in the darkness and saw something white, like the bones of a hand holding onto her, pulling her back down. She screamed, "She's got me!" and fainted.

Outside the graveyard, the polite girl heard the scream and ran back to the field to get her father and brothers. The men were already walking home for the night and met her on the road. She told them what had happened, and they hurried to the graveyard with one candle-lantern to light their way. Inside the graveyard, the polite girl led the men and boys all the way back through the trees to the grave of the old woman. There lay the body of the sassy girl, fallen over the grave. When the men lifted the girl she woke up.

Everyone laughed. When the sassy girl had bent over and stuck the fork in the ground, she had caught the bottom of her own dress. It was only the fork that had grabbed her and held her to the old witch's grave.

THE WHITE WOLF

The wide open plains of Texas are lonely and empty in many parts. You can get on your horse and ride and ride and not see anyone else. If you take along your bedroll and sleep out under the stars, you may see someone else you're not too sure you wanted to see. You just might see the White Wolf.

Every once in a while there's an animal born, a cow or a horse or a dog, that's all white. No other color, just white. And people think those animals are special. They put them in zoos sometimes for people to see. Maybe it's just by accident that those animals are such a ghostly color with red, red eyes. Maybe. Or maybe not.

A long time ago there was a wagon train crossing the plains with many families going west looking for a new place to live. Nobody wanted much to live on the Texas plains. There wasn't enough grass or water or trees. So mostly they passed on by and went further west. But in this wagon train there was a family with a boy who was very sick. They had to stop and stay in one place, waiting for the

boy to get better, while the rest of the wagons went on west.

The boy slept in the wagon mostly, but one night he asked to sleep outside under the stars. So his mother and father let him. During the night, when the moon came up and it was easy to see things, the boy awoke suddenly. In the dim light he could see something sitting not far from his bedroll, staring at him with red, red eyes.

At first the boy was scared. But the thing didn't ever move and the boy began to think maybe he wasn't really seeing it. Maybe his high fever made him think he saw it. He fell asleep. When he woke again the moon was higher and the thing was sitting closer, staring at him with red, red eyes. He was afraid for a minute, but the thing didn't ever move. The boy fell asleep again, feeling bad from the fever.

When he awoke again the moon was at the top of the sky and the thing was sitting right beside him looking down at him with red, red eyes. "It's a dog," said the boy, "just a big, white dog." The thing leaned down and licked him on the face. The boy laughed and fell asleep. But he never woke up again. The fever was too much, and he died. 'Way off on the nearby mesa a wolf howled long and low.

The next day his family buried the boy under a mound of sand with a cactus growing on top. As the wagon rolled on they talked about the tracks in the dust around the bedroll. From high on the mesa something watched the wagon go.

Year after year, when wagons passed the same

place and stopped to spend the night, people would see the ghostly white form walking the dusty plains near the wagons. It never came close but somehow it seemed lonely. Once, a wagon stopped beside the grave, and the people saw small, white bones sticking out of the sand. Suddenly, over the top of the mound of sand came a huge, white wolf snarling at them. Those people left as fast as they could go.

Some people said the White Wolf protected the boy's grave. Some people said the White Wolf had killed the boy in the sandy grave. But as the years went by the people began to say something else.

They began to say the White Wolf was the ghost of the boy.

Around the dusty stone walls at the ruins of Fort Phantom Hill, some say the ghost for which the old fort was named was once a boy on a wagon train— and now was a great White Wolf with red, red eyes.

THE CHANGELINGS

"Hip! Hop! Skip!" sing the goblins and trolls as they dance around the fire at night. "Hip! Hop! Skip!" Then the goblins call for their servants to serve them their supper of rags and twigs and jelly and jam. And who are the goblins' servants? Why, boys and girls like you and me! How did the goblins get their servants?

Ah, that's another story!

Sometimes when a human child is born the goblins and trolls hear about it and come sneaking at night whispering, "Hip! Hop! Skip! Hip! Hop! Skip!" They come down the chimney or in through the coal bin and steal the human child. They take it and raise it and make it their servant, and in its place they leave a goblin baby or a troll baby that cries and complains and grows up doing bad things. And because the baby seems to its parents to have changed from a good child to a bad child it is called a changeling."

"Hip! Hop! Skip!"

One night a young mother and father were sound asleep in their big, warm bed beside the fireplace. Their pretty new baby was sound asleep in his crib. Then, in the deep of the night, the fire gave a "Crack!" and the young father awoke.

There in the dim red light of the fire he saw a

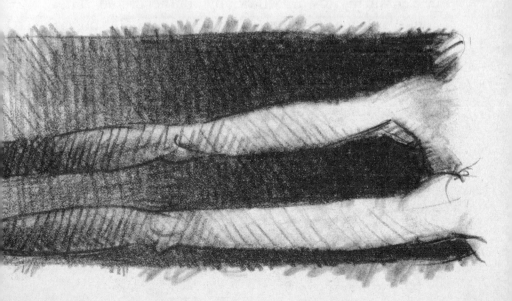

goblin sitting in a chair by the fire warming his feet with claws on them. The goblin's teeth were long and pointy, his ears were tall and pointy, and out of the back of his pants came a long, pointy tail.

The goblin wiggled his toes and warmed his hands with claws on them. He drummed his toes on the stone floor in front of the fireplace. *Clickitty-click,* went the claws on his toes, *clickitty-click.* His tail twitched back and forth as he warmed his toes. *Twitchitty-twitch,* went his tail, *twitchitty-twitch!*

The young father was so scared he couldn't move.

Outside the house he heard the goblins dancing, whispering "Hip! Hop! Skip!" They danced around the house. "Hip! Hop! Skip!" One of the trolls called down the chimney, "Bring out the baby!"

Whispering, whining, howling, he said, "Bring out the baby!"

The goblin sat still in the chair but he reached out his arms toward the baby in the cradle. The goblin's arms got longer and longer. He never moved from the chair but his arms got longer and longer. Closer and closer to the young father's bed, closer and closer to the baby's crib, the goblin's arms got longer and longer.

The goblin's arms reached all the way past the fireplace, all the way across the room, all the way to the baby's cradle.

Just then the baby turned a little in his sleep. The little gold cross the young father had put on a necklace around the baby's neck shone in the fire-light.

Goblins hate crosses.

The goblin's arms got shorter and shorter and shorter.

Down the chimney called the troll, "Bring out the baby!"

"I can't," said the goblin in a whisper that sounded like mice walking in the wall. "He's wearing the I-hate-it thing."

The goblin walked into the fireplace and climbed up the chimney with the smoke.

Outside the young father could hear the goblins dancing away.

"Hip! Hop! Skip!" They whispered and whined and howled. "Hip! Hop! Skip!" Then they were gone.

The goblins would have to find someone else to serve them supper when he grew up. "Hip! Hop! Skip!"

WHAM! SLAM!
JENNY-MO-JAM!

Once there were a little boy and a little girl whose mother knew some magic spells; she had even taught them a few. As the two grew older, people told them that their grandmother was an evil witch who had a magic ball she used to hunt down children. The brother and sister wondered if these scary stories could be true. They begged their mother to let them go through the forest to the home of the old woman who had raised her.

"No, dear children," said their mother, "you must not go there. No one who has ever spent the night in that forest returned!" The children assured their mother that no harm would come to them, because they also knew some magic spells and would be sure to be back before dark.

Finally the brother put his twelve dogs in their pen and told his mother that if anything happened to him and his sister he would give a special whistle that only the dogs could hear. If the mother heard the dogs barking for no reason, she should let them out of the pen so they could run to the rescue. The children kissed their mother good-bye and left.

It was still early afternoon when the children started out for the grandmother's house in the forest, and after a long walk they saw her working in her garden. All her plants were very tall and of very strange shapes and colors. When the old woman saw the children, she clapped her hands with glee and asked them their names.

"I'm Jenny," said the girl.

"I'm Mo," said the boy.

The old woman asked them to come inside and meet her own two children, who were about the same size and age as Jenny and Mo, but whose ears seemed just a little too pointed and furry and whose teeth were just a little too long and sharp.

The children played in the yard, but the old woman's kids didn't seem to know any of the right games. The children talked to the old woman and were surprised to see the sun suddenly go down. They hadn't realized how late it was. All too soon it was dark, and they had to stay the night in the old woman's house.

The grandmother told all four children to eat the cornpone that was on the table and to go upstairs and get ready for bed. In the meantime, she set a great iron kettle on the hearth and built a fire underneath it. She filled the kettle with water and soon it began to boil. Then the old woman went upstairs and showed the children where to sleep. To her own children she gave a dark bedsheet to sleep under; to Jenny and Mo she gave a white bedsheet. Pretty soon the two wild-looking kids were asleep and snoring in a grunting sort of way. Even

Jenny fell asleep. But Mo was worried and stayed awake.

Downstairs the old woman took a sharp knife out of her belt and began to sharpen it on a whetstone. *Skriiiitch... skriiiitch...* went the knife.

The witch called up to the children, "Are you asleep yet?"

"Not me," said Mo. "When I'm at home and I can't sleep, my mother gives me the fiddle to play."

The old woman brought up a fiddle and the boy sat on the floor and played and played. The witch sat on the bottom step of the stairs and sharpened her knife. *Skriiiitch... skriiiitch...* The boy played the sweetest tune he knew, one that his mother sang him and his sister to sleep with, and soon he heard the old woman snoring at the foot of the steps.

The boy put down the fiddle and woke his sister. They fluffed up their feather pillows and laid them on the pallet where they had been sleeping to make it look like they were still there. Then they traded the bedsheets so that the white sheet was over the wild-looking kids. Jenny and Mo tiptoed past the sleeping witch and ran down the dark moonlit path toward their own home.

Pretty soon the witch woke and went to the white sheet and killed the children under it. When she lit a candle and saw that she had killed her own kids, she was howling mad. She ran to her trunk and took out the magic glass ball. She flew to the front door and rolled it down one path. It rolled away, but came rolling back after a few minutes. She knew they had not gone that way.

She rolled the ball down another path and it kept going. When it didn't come back soon, she followed it, carrying with her a large axe from her shed.

Jenny and Mo heard the magic ball rumbling behind them and knew what the sound must mean.

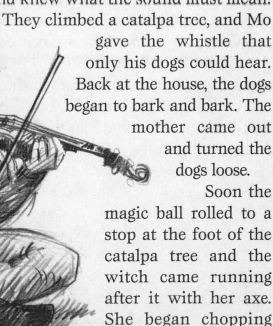

They climbed a catalpa tree, and Mo gave the whistle that only his dogs could hear. Back at the house, the dogs began to bark and bark. The mother came out and turned the dogs loose.

Soon the magic ball rolled to a stop at the foot of the catalpa tree and the witch came running after it with her axe. She began chopping down the tree, chanting, "Wham! Slam! Jenny-Mo-Jam! Wham! Slam! Jenny-Mo-Jam!" The chips flew as the axe cut into the trunk of the tree.

Every time she sang her chant, Mo sang another spell: "Catalpa tree, when the axe goes 'Chop,' grow big at the bottom and little at the top!" Every time a chip fell another one grew back.

"Wham! Slam! Jenny-Mo-Jam! Wham! Slam! Jenny-Mo-Jam!"

"Catalpa tree, when the axe goes 'Chop,' grow big at the bottom and little at the top!" The catalpa tree stood firm.

It wasn't too long before those twelve dogs came running to help. They barked and jumped around and bit the old witch, but she swung her axe with one hand and her knife with the other. She killed eleven of the dogs, but the last dog jumped at her throat and sank his teeth in and killed her.

When Jenny and Mo climbed down they took the big knife and cut out the witch's heart. They rubbed the heart on the noses of the dead dogs, and they all jumped back to life. The dogs and the children walked home and met their mother just as the sun came up.

THE KI'IN SPIRITS

It was at the beginning of time, in the forest of the Ancient Land, that there lived the most evil of beings, the Ki'in. These Ki'in were spirit-things that came in the night and ate the souls of men and women. Then they lived in the empty bodies of their victims, acting as if they were the people themselves. Even the close kinfolk of the victims would never suspect that the body they were talking to was no longer lived in by their loved one, but was like an empty grass hut that someone evil had moved into.

There were two ways to tell the difference between real people and the Ki'in walking about in their stolen human bodies. The Ki'in went out in their bodies only at night. They left the empty bodies sleeping in the daylight, while the Ki'in hid in spirit form in some difficult-to-find place of safety. If your kinsman always wanted to sleep by day and fish or hunt by night, that was a warning that perhaps he was a Ki'in. Also, while out at night, the Ki'in ate only things that were still alive: they could not stand cooked food because fire was their only

enemy on the earth. If your kinsman ate fish and bugs that were still alive and wiggling, that was a sure sign he was a Ki'in.

One night a boy was sitting in front of his hut, and one of his uncles came along with another man. "Let's go fishing, boy," said the uncle. The boy smiled and joined them in the moonlight, walking down the riverbank to the fishing boats cut from the trunks of trees that grew in the forest of the Ancient Land. The three poled their way off the riverbank and began to paddle along the grassy marsh at the edge of the slow-moving river.

"Let's catch some bait first," said the uncle. The boy stepped out of the boat into the shallow water and caught a frog. He gave it to the uncle. When the boy's back was turned, he heard the uncle say, *"Gulp ... Oh, that one got away."*

This seemed strange to the boy because he had not heard a splash, like the sound of a frog jumping from the boat. He caught another frog and gave it to his uncle's friend. When the boy's back was turned the other man said, *"Gulp ... Oh, I dropped that one."*

Now the boy was afraid. His uncle and the other man were Ki'in. Even though the Ki'in were hard to discover, normal people knew about them, and this boy had figured out what was happening.

"I'll go behind this fallen log and look for really big frogs," the boy said, and he quickly stepped into the high grass, out of sight of the Ki'in in the boat.

When he got to the other side of the log he said, "Here's a big one ... *gulp* ... he was delicious."

When the Ki'in heard this, they looked at each other and said to themselves, "He's one of us."

"Wait," said the boy, "and I'll find another big one." Then after a pause he said, "In the daytime while this boy's body sleeps, I hide in a little basket with a lid. Where do you hide?"

The uncle laughed. "I thought all the spirit-things hid with *us*. I did not know any of our number hid in a basket."

"Oh," said the boy, "there are many of us who hide in baskets."

The other man laughed, too. "That is a silly place to hide," said the man. "We hide in the top of the bamboo stalk beside the water buffalo pen, in a hole that bees made for their nest."

"That is a good place," said the boy.

Then the boy bent down to a little frog he saw sitting on the log. "Little frog," he whispered, "These men are really Ki'in and they want to eat you. If you will help me I will leave you alone."

"Very well," said the frog, because frogs can talk if they have anything very important to say.

"When the men call for me, say 'I think I have a big one; wait just a moment.'"

"Very well," said the frog.

The boy crept away through the grass to the riverbank and ran back to his house.

"What's taking you so long?" said the uncle back in the boat.

"I think I have a big one," said the little frog in his deepest voice. "Wait just a moment."

After a few minutes the other Ki'in in the boat

called out, "What's taking you so long, boy?"

"I think I have a big one," croaked the little frog. "Wait just a moment."

After a little while the men became suspicious and paddled the boat around the log. The little frog jumped in the water with a splash and was gone. The men looked around for more frogs, but all the frogs were hiding. The little frog had warned them.

The sun was about to rise, so the men gave up and went back to their huts to sleep.

Just at sunrise the boy awoke in his own hut and ran outside to the water buffalo pen. Hiding in the underbrush, he watched the top of the bamboo stalk. Sure enough here came little things with wings, almost invisible against the blue sky, flying in from all directions. They flew into a bee-hole in the bamboo just before the morning sunlight hit the tall bamboo stalk.

The boy got his father's curved knife and chopped the bamboo down. The bee-hole buzzed with angry voices but the boy didn't listen. He plugged the bee-hole with a stick and cut away the one long segment of the stalk containing the bee-hole. He ran to the cooking fire in front of his hut and threw the bamboo into the flame.

The bamboo stalk burned up, and all the Ki'in burned up, too. At least, we hope it was all of them. Maybe it wasn't.

If a friend of yours eats live frogs, maybe it wasn't.

Maybe it wasn't.

WHO'S FOLLOWING ME?

One dark night, a little boy had stayed in the park too long. It was late, and his mother was going to be mad. It was dark, and it was a long, long way to his house. He started walking slowly out of the park.

He walked slowly along. Each time he took a step, he heard something behind him take a step, walking slowly along. He stopped and looked back. There was no one there. "Who's following me?" he said.

He walked a little faster. Each time he heard his shoe hit the sidewalk, he heard something else make a sound, like someone behind him taking a step—walking a little faster. He stopped and looked back. There was no one there. "Who's following me?" he said.

He started to run just a little. Each time his foot hit the ground, he heard something else, like feet behind him hitting the ground—starting to run just a little. He stopped and looked back. There was no one there...that he could see.

He started to run fast. Each step he took, he

heard someone behind him taking a step—starting to run fast. He didn't stop. He didn't look back. He ran and he ran and he ran.

He ran to his block and he ran to his yard and he ran to his porch. On the porch he stopped and looked back. There was no one there. But when he took another step he heard that noise again. He looked down at his shoe.

The sole was coming off his old shoe, and every time he took a step, the loose sole flapped and made a noise. He had been running from himself!

Bloody Mary, Bloody Mary

Once there was a queen. She was a mean queen. She commanded and she demanded. And if you didn't do what she told you, she chopped off your head, and then you were dead.

Soon she gained fame, and people gave her the name "Bloody Mary."

Then she died, but nobody cried for Bloody Mary.

Then people forgot what she was or was not, Bloody Mary.

Then centuries passed, and at long last, kids would tell the story about the queen that was gory, Bloody Mary.

And some kids said that, just like before, if you called her name, you could see her once more. If you stood in front of a mirror in the middle of the night, and you looked at yourself, and you turned out the light, and you said the words that were just exactly right, you'd see her in your mirror, and she'd give you such a fright! Bloody Mary!

One little girl loved to hear scary stories. She and her friends would tell them and squeal. But she

never thought that any of the stuff that anybody told in those stories was real. Then she heard about Bloody Mary, and she learned the words to chant. She stood at her mirror, and she said, "Oh, I can't."

But it was such fun to be scared. "It can't hurt anything," she thought. And she completely forgot all the things she'd been taught by her mom and her preacher and her grade school teacher.

"I do believe in Bloody Mary," she whispered as she looked at herself in the mirror. "I do believe in Bloody Mary," she repeated, and she leaned over, nearer and nearer.

"I do believe in Bloody Mary," she said, in the darkness and gloom. "I do believe in Bloody Mary," she said, all alone in her room.

Then she looked at herself, and her hair was a mess, and where she got those clothes she just couldn't guess. There in the mirror her skin looked cruddy, and she held up her hands and her hands were all bloody. Those eyes weren't her eyes, they were gleaming and scary! The face in her mirror was Bloody Mary!

The little girl screamed and let out a yelp. She tried to step back, she tried to call for help. The queen leaned out of the mirror. The girl yelled, but no one could hear her.

Bloody Mary grabbed for the little girl's throat with her bloody hands in her velvet coat.

The girl hit the switch and turned on the light.

And stood there alone, in her room, in the night.

Red Velvet Ribbon

Long ago and far away lived a fancy rich man with a big black silk hat and a fine silk tie. He went out walking every day, hoping some pretty girl would see him and fall in love with him and become his bride.

He met a lot of ladies in the park, but he was just a little too stuck-up for them. They didn't like him very much.

He met a lot of ladies down by the riverside where people go rowing in boats, but he bragged just a little too much for them. They didn't like him very much.

He even tried visiting the graveyard. There he met a pretty lady in a pretty white dress with a red velvet ribbon tied around her neck. He admired the red velvet ribbon, and as they talked, he reached up and touched it.

"That's my red velvet ribbon," she said, "and you can't ever take it off."

Time passed. Spring became summer, summer became autumn. The rich man with the big black silk hat and the fine silk tie fell in love with the

pretty lady in the pretty white dress with the red velvet ribbon tied around her neck.

At their wedding, he wore his big black silk hat and his fine silk tie, and she wore a lovely wedding dress—and her red velvet ribbon around her neck.

On their honeymoon, he touched her lovely neck and touched the red velvet ribbon, but she said, "You can't ever take it off."

The next year they had a baby. They were both very happy, but the fancy rich man was beginning to be bothered by that red velvet ribbon. He could buy anything he wanted. He could afford anything he wanted. But he couldn't take that red velvet ribbon off his wife's neck.

Finally, when the baby was one year old, the fancy rich man couldn't stand it any longer. While his pretty wife was taking a nap and the baby was sound asleep in her crib, he crept into the room and sneaked up on his sleeping wife.

Very gently, he untied the red velvet ribbon.

Very gently, he removed the red velvet ribbon.

Very gently, her head rolled to the side, rolled off the bed, and fell to the floor!

WYLIE AND THE HAIRY MAN

Deep in the swamp, a boy named Wylie lived with his Momma, who knew magic spells and secret charms. Wylie loved his Momma, and his Momma loved Wylie. Wylie's Poppa was dead and gone. He'd been killed many years before in a fight with the Hairy Man who lived in the swamp. The Hairy Man knew magic, too, but all his spells were bad spells. The Hairy Man knew secret charms, too, but all his charms were evil charms.

Everyone was afraid of the Hairy Man, but he never left the swamp. The Hairy Man himself wasn't afraid of anything—except dogs. That old Hairy Man sure didn't like dogs. So whenever Wylie went into the swamp to gather wood or pick berries, he would take his dogs along. That old Hairy Man sure didn't like dogs.

One day Wylie's Momma sent him into the swamp to gather wood, but she told him to tie up his dogs. He wasn't going very far from the shack, and if he took the dogs, he would just be gone longer. The dogs would chase rabbits, and Wylie and the dogs would just play and play, and the wood gathering wouldn't get done. So she told him to tie up the dogs.

Before he left, his Momma called Wylie into the kitchen. "See this here glass of milk?" she said, "I put a spell on it. If that old Hairy Man starts to bother you, this milk will turn as red as blood and I'll set your dogs loose. That way you'll be safe."

Wylie set out to gather wood for the supper fire. He wandered further and further from the shack, looking for dry wood for the fire. He got so far into the swamp that the Hairy Man smelled him coming, and when Wylie looked up from picking up a piece of wood, there he stood! That old Hairy Man!

"Hellooo, Wyyylie," said the Hairy Man. His voice sounded like Wylie's Momma's grinder. "How are youuu?"

"I'm fine, Mr. Hairy Man," Wylie said with a gulp. "How are you?" Wylie began to back away.

"I'm huuungry," said the Hairy Man, moving toward Wylie.

"What've you got in mind to eat, Mr. Hairy Man?" asked Wylie, backing away further.

"Youuu," said the Hairy Man, moving closer.

Back at the shack, the glass of milk on the table turned as red as blood. Wylie's Momma knew that Wylie was in trouble, and she set the dogs loose. The dogs could smell that old Hairy Man, and they ran into the swamp, barking.

"What's that noooise?" asked the Hairy Man.

"Them are my dogs, Mr. Hairy Man," said Wylie.

"Wyyylie…" said the Hairy Man, "Goodbyyye!"

The dogs came crashing through the underbrush and chased that old Hairy Man about a hundred miles. Wylie went home with the firewood.

On another day, Wylie's Momma sent him out in the swamp to pick berries. He tied up his dogs so they wouldn't follow him, and his Momma put another glass of milk out with a spell on it. Wylie went to pick berries, carrying a big bucket.

Wylie wandered further and further from the shack looking for berry canes with ripe berries on them. He got so far into the swamp that the Hairy Man smelled him coming. When Wylie looked up from a cane of ripe berries, there he stood! That old Hairy Man!

"Hellooo, Wyyylie," said the Hairy Man, and his voice sounded like claws scratching on a screen door. "Whaaat's new?"

"Not much," said Wylie, backing away. "What's new with you?"

Back at the shack, that glass of milk with a magic spell on it turned as red as blood, but Wylie's Momma was outside beating the rugs. She didn't see it, so she didn't set the dogs loose.

"I'm still huuungry," said the Hairy Man, coming closer to Wylie.

"Want some berries?" asked Wylie, throwing

the bucket at the Hairy Man.

"No, thaaanks," said the Hairy Man. "I've got something biiigger in mind."

Wylie climbed a cypress tree, and the Hairy Man came slowly over to the knees at the bottom of the tree and looked up at him.

"I'm going to eat youuu, Wyyylie," said the Hairy Man.

Now, those dogs ought to have been there by then, but Wylie couldn't hear them barking.

"Before you eat me, Mr. Hairy Man..."

"Yesss, Wyyylie..."

"Before you eat me, would you show me how good you can do magic spells?"

The Hairy Man puffed out his chest and acted real proud at that. "Suuure, Wyyylie," said that old Hairy Man. "What shall I dooo?"

"Well, sir," said Wylie, "could you make a big bunch of rope just appear out of nowhere?"

"Suuure," said the Hairy Man standing at the foot of the cypress tree. "Rope, rope, lots of rooope," said the Hairy Man, and suddenly there were ropes hanging all over the place, off the

trees and piled on the ground.

"Now I can get away," yelled Wylie up in the tree. He started to swing from one of the ropes like he was escaping. "You'd have to make all the rope in the swamp vanish to catch me now!"

"Aaall the rope in the swaaamp," growled the Hairy Man, "Vaaanish!"

All the rope on the ground vanished.

All the rope in the trees vanished.

The rope holding up Wylie's pants vanished, and he nearly lost his pants.

All the rope tying up his dogs vanished, and they came crashing through the underbrush, howling and barking.

"Wyyylie," said the Hairy Man, "Goodbyyye!"

And those dogs chased that old Hairy Man about two hundred miles through the swamp.

Wylie held up his pants with one hand, picked up the bucket in the other hand, and walked home.

After that, no matter how long it took to run his errands in the swamp, no matter how much those dogs played, and no matter how late he came in from his chores at night, Wylie's Momma didn't ever make him tie up his dogs again!

MARRIED TO A GHOST

Not long after the world began, the People built their lodges beside the great water in what we call the Pacific Northwest. In one village, the young chief was named Lone Feather. He met a pretty young woman who was named Robin because that bird had sung outside her father's lodge on the morning she was born. Lone Feather and Robin planned to be married when the springtime came and the snows that blew down from the Cascade Mountains began to melt.

In the last cold days of winter, Lone Feather became very ill and had a high fever. At last, his spirit left his body and walked down the spirit trail to the Land of the Dead. Robin and all the People were sad.

The People went in canoes and took the body of the chief to a burial island. They placed the body on a high platform of poles. Then they left quickly. No one dared to stay on a burial island very long.

Springtime came, and Robin was still very sad. One night she had a dream. In her dream, Lone Feather came to her and told her that he had not found peace in the Land of the Dead because he missed her so much.

Robin told her father of her dream. He agreed to help her. They paddled their canoe up the Great River to the most distant and most sacred burial island. No one ever went to this island any more. It had become the secret place of the Dead.

As the night came, Robin and her father paddled through darkness and thick fog toward the Land of the Dead. In the distance they heard the drum being played, and they heard the Dead singing and dancing. They sounded very happy. Robin's father let her out of the canoe and paddled away down the river.

Robin walked through the fog to the village of the Dead. She was welcomed at first, until the Dead began to see that she was still alive. "No one who is alive is allowed in the Land of the Dead," they said. Then Lone Feather saw her and they ran to each other. They were very happy to be together. Lone Feather looked even more well and handsome than he had when he was alive.

All the Dead liked Lone Feather. He talked them into letting Robin stay and be one of them. They sang and danced all night long. Just before dawn, all the Dead went to their lodges. Robin and Lone Feather went to his lodge and laid down beside each other on a sleeping mat. The robins began to sing as the sun came up.

The young girl slept, but she was not used to sleeping in the daytime, and she woke up when the sun was high. Beside her, the young chief was nothing

but a skeleton. She jumped up and ran outside. All around were skeletons, each lying where one of the Dead had stood or sat or danced too long and the rising sun had caught them. Robin was afraid. She sat alone all day.

When darkness fell, the Dead rose again and began to sing and dance. Lone Feather came to her, and Robin was again happy. After many months had passed, Robin and Lone Feather had a son. They were all very happy, but Robin wished she could go back to the Land of the Living and show her new son to her father and mother.

All the Dead told her not to go back to the Land of the Living. "If you do go," said one wise old woman, "you must not allow anyone to look upon the child for ten days." Another said, "If you go back to the Land of the Living, you might not be able to return here." Still another said, "If you go back, the Living may think you are an evil ghost come back from the dead. They may not welcome you back."

In spite of all the good advice from her friends among the Dead, Robin went back home. When the sun was high and the Dead were all skeletons, she wrapped the baby in a blanket and paddled a canoe back to her village.

At her village, the People did not trust her. The People thought she was an evil ghost. No one ever came back from the Land of the Dead; what business did *she* have coming back?

Robin's father and mother were happy to see her again. She hid in their lodge so the other People would not be angered by the sight of her. Robin's mother wanted to see the baby. Robin told her they must wait ten days before the baby could be brought out into the sunlight. Robin's mother did not like that. She became impatient and could not wait to see her grandson.

One bright day, while Robin was asleep, the grandmother opened the blanket and looked inside. The baby was a skeleton. The grandmother dropped the baby and the little bones scattered all over the lodge. Day and night, the bones were just bones.

Sadly, Robin gathered the bones and canoed back to the Land of the Dead. There the little bones were a baby again when the sun went down. The three were very happy: Lone Feather, Robin, and their son.

And the Dead met in tribal council and declared that no one may ever again pass back and forth between the Land of the Living and the Land of the Dead.

The Tiger's Eyes

One day while hunting in the forest, a man killed a big monkey called a gibbon to take home to his wife and child and his little sister who lived with them. The gibbon was good meat, and they would have plenty to eat for many days. The man saw the forest, he saw the gibbon, he saw good meat for many days. He did not see one thing. He did not see the tiger's eyes.

The tiger's eyes looked out from a hiding place in the deep forest. The tiger watched the man. He knew that, for a tiger, the man was good meat for many days. The tiger jumped out of the bushes and killed the man and ate him.

The tiger sat down and licked his lips. He looked at the dead gibbon, and he looked at the clothes the man had been wearing. The tiger had an idea.

The tiger put on the man's clothes. He picked up the man's bow and arrows in one paw and the gibbon in the other paw. He stood up on his back legs and said, "Now I am a man."

He walked back to the man's village and went into the house that smelled like the man he had eaten. He greeted the man's wife and said, "I am your husband."

"Oh," said the foolish wife, "I see you got a monkey." She began to fix the monkey for supper, and she never even looked at the tiger's eyes. Now, the man's little sister looked more closely at the tiger and saw that he had fur on his hands and he had a tail. She looked him in the eyes and knew that this was not her brother.

"This is not your husband," the little sister whispered to the wife. "He has tiger's eyes!"

"Oh, Yurr," said the wife, for that is what she called her husband's sister, "He's just being silly." And the wife went on making supper. The tiger's wife cut the gibbon into four pieces: one for the tiger she thought was her husband, one for their little son, one for herself, and one for Yurr, the little sister.

The tiger picked up his piece of meat and ate it raw.

"This is not your husband," Yurr whispered to the foolish wife. "He eats like a tiger!"

"Oh, he's just being silly," said the tiger's wife and she went on making supper. *Crunch, crunch, crunch* went the bones of the gibbon as the tiger chewed them up.

After supper, everyone went to bed. The tiger and his wife slept on a mat by the cooking fire. The little son slept on a mat by the door. Yurr climbed up to the storage floor above the main room of the house and slept on a mat where the peppers were hanging to dry.

Down below, in the darkness, the tiger ate the foolish wife. *Crunch, crunch, crunch* went the bones as the tiger chewed them up. Yurr got off her mat and listened from the top step of the ladder. Down below, in the darkness, the tiger ate the foolish wife's son. *Crunch, crunch, crunch* went the bones as the tiger chewed them up

The tiger licked his lips and sat down below in the darkness.

After a while, the tiger came to the foot of the ladder and called up to Yurr, "Sister, come down."

"Oh, no," called Yurr back to him. "If you want to see me, you have to come up." She hurried to the farthest place in the storage room and hid behind a string of red peppers that were drying. Then she had an idea!

Yurr took some of the red peppers and put them in a grinding bowl and ground them into red powder. Then she took her washing bowl and put the red pepper powder into the water. Just then, the tiger reached the top step of the ladder and looked up into the storage floor. Yurr threw the pepper-water in the tiger's eyes.

The tiger growled and dropped to the ground. He ran to the river to wash his eyes. Yurr climbed down the ladder to run away, but when she got to the door of the house, the tiger was already coming back. She grabbed another bowl of water from beside the cooking fire and ran back up the ladder.

As Yurr huddled in the farthest place of the storage floor she began to cry. "What shall I do?" she cried.

Under the grass roof of the house, there was a little bird's nest. The little bird said, "What is wrong?"

"My brother has become a tiger," Yurr answered, "and has eaten my sister-in-law and her son. Little bird, fly to my people and tell them to come and help me! Hurry, little bird, and I and my people will feed you and all your people forever."

The little bird agreed and flew out the smoke-hole over the cooking fire. The tiger came into the house and paced in a circle around the foot of the ladder. After a while, the tiger came to the foot of the ladder and called up to Yurr. "Sister, come down."

"Oh, no," called Yurr back to him. "If you want to see me, you have to come up." She ground more peppers from the string that was drying above her and put the red powder into the water she had gotten from beside the cooking fire.

The tiger climbed the ladder again and the tiger's eyes looked over the storage floor toward Yurr. Once again, Yurr threw pepper-water into the tiger's eyes. The tiger howled and growled and snarled and jumped to the ground. He ran back to the river to wash his eyes again.

While the tiger was at the river, Yurr's people came from her house. "The little bird came and told us that our brother is dead. Where is the tiger?" they asked.

"Down at the river washing his eyes," said Yurr. As she explained what had happened, her brothers dug a tiger-trap right at the front door to the house.

They covered the tiger-trap with a grass mat from the house, and they all stood around it, with Yurr at the far side of the trap.

Back from the river came the tiger.

"Welcome, brother," said Yurr to the tiger. "See, our family has come for a late visit. Will you ask them in?"

"Come in," said the tiger, thinking of the great meal he would have if he ate all these people.

"After you, brother," said Yurr, and the tiger walked across the mat on his back legs.

The mat gave way and the tiger fell into the tiger-trap. Yurr's brothers killed him with their spears.

Forever after, even today, the people feed the little bird and her children, and keep them and their nests in the people's houses. And everyone remembers the tiger's eyes.

Blood-Red Cedar

Once there were a young man and a young woman who got married and lived in a house on a hill. The woman brought with her a hope chest made out of blood-red cedar. In it she kept her linens and things, where the moths wouldn't hurt them. When her first child was born, it was a little boy. His skin was as white as linen, and his healthy lips were as red as blood-red cedar. They named the boy Will.

When Will was a boy, his mother died of a fever. Will's father knew he couldn't raise the boy alone. He married a widow-woman who had a younger daughter named Marjorie. Will and Marjorie loved each other like brother and sister, but Marjorie's mother hated Will and wished he would die.

One day there were apples picked fresh and brought into the house. Will came in from chores and wanted one. The evil stepmother took him to his mother's blood-red cedar chest to get the silver knife to peel the apples with. When Will bent over to reach into the chest, the stepmother slammed the lid.

Will's head fell off into the chest.

The stepmother laughed and laughed, but she knew she would have to hide her crime. She set Will up in a chair in the kitchen and set his head on properly. Then she tied a napkin around his neck as if he were about to eat. She put an apple in one of his hands and the silver knife in the other.

When Marjorie came into the house, she saw the apples. She asked if she could have one. "Share your brother's apple," said her evil mother. When Marjorie asked Will for a piece of his apple, Will did not answer. "Just hit him, then," said the evil woman.

When Marjorie hit her brother, his head fell off, and Marjorie thought it was her fault. She cried and cried. Now, the woman said she would hide Marjorie's crime, even though Marjorie had not killed her brother.

The woman cooked Will in a pot and served him for supper. She told Will's father that Will had gone away to live with an aunt. Marjorie didn't eat that night. Marjorie only cried.

After supper, little Marjorie gathered up all the bones, wrapped them in her linen napkin, and buried them under the red cedar tree in the yard. A strong wind blew and the cedar tree shook.

Then the cedar gave off its red powdery pollen as if it were springtime. The red powder whirled around the tree in the wind. It looked as if the tree were on fire. It looked as if the tree were red with blood. The tree shook and a little bird flew out of its branches.

The bird landed in another tree and began to sing.

My mother, she murdered me.
My father, he ate me.
But my loving sister Marjorie
Put all my bones beneath a tree.
And I came back to sing on high,
Oh, what a pretty bird am I.

Marjorie laughed and clapped her hands. She knew that the bird was her brother. There was magic in the cedar tree.

Marjorie went back into the house.

The pretty bird flew over the fields and forest and into the village. The bird landed on the window of the metalsmith's house. The smith was making a chain of silver to take to the fair and sell. The bird began to sing.

My mother, she murdered me.
My father, he ate me.
But my loving sister Marjorie
Put all my bones beneath a tree.
And I came back to sing on high,
Oh, what a pretty bird am I.

The metalsmith looked up. "That tune is the most beautiful song I have ever heard. If you will sing it again for my wife, I will give you this silver chain."

The bird agreed. The smith called his wife, and with their arms about each other, they listened to the song. The smith put the silver chain around the bird's neck.

The pretty bird flew over the houses and roofs and

landed on the windowsill of the bootmaker's shop. The bootmaker was making a fine pair of boots to take to the fair and sell. The bird began to sing.

My mother, she murdered me.
My father, he ate me.
But my loving sister Marjorie
Put all my bones beneath a tree.
And I came back to sing on high,
Oh, what a pretty bird am I.

The bootmaker put down his tools and said, "That is the finest song I ever heard a bird sing. If you will sing it for me again, I will give you this fine pair of boots."

The bird agreed and sang the song again. Even though the boots seemed quite large, they somehow

fit the little bird perfectly, and he flew away.

The pretty bird flew over the river and over the millpond and landed in the windowsill of the grinding mill. Men were just finishing putting in a new stone to grind the corn. The old millstone, as round and flat as a giant's pancake, sat against the wall. The bird began to sing.

> My mother, she murdered me.
> My father, he ate me.
> But my loving sister Marjorie
> Put all my bones beneath a tree.
> And I came back to sing on high,
> Oh, what a pretty bird am I.

All the men agreed that the song was the most unusual one they had ever heard. They asked the bird to sing it again. "If only you will sing that song again, we will give you the old grindstone from the mill. You can build your nest in the hole in the center."

The bird agreed and sang again. The men lifted the grindstone. Though the stone weighed many pounds, the bird put its head through the hole in the center of the stone and flew away with it.

The pretty bird flew to Marjorie's house and sat above the front door. He began to sing.

> My mother, she murdered me.
> My father, he ate me.
> But my loving sister Marjorie
> Put all my bones beneath a tree.
> And I came back to sing on high,
> Oh, what a pretty bird am I.

Marjorie knew it was her brother singing, and she ran outside. The bird bowed its head and the silver chain fell off. It fell around Marjorie's neck and made her even prettier than she was before.

The father heard the bird singing, and he came from the barn. The bird picked up its feet one by one and kicked off the boots. When the boots hit the ground, they were just the right size to fit his father's feet. He took off his old boots and put on the new ones.

The evil stepmother came up from the root cellar to see what bird was singing.

Marjorie and her stepfather told the evil woman about their gifts. She asked the bird, "What have you brought for me?"

The bird bowed very low, and the heavy millstone fell from its shoulders. It fell on the evil woman and crushed her.

The bird flew down to the millstone. When he landed, there was a burst of fire, or of cedar pollen, or a splash of blood. There was Will, standing on the millstone, well and whole.

Will told them both what had happened. The three lived happily. And when Will's father married the miller's sister later, she was a kind and loving stepmother to them all.

SPIRIT OF FIRE

The spirit of Fire is a powerful spirit. She buries her enemies in dark volcanic lava. When an army fought against her favorite king, she sent lava to cover them, and only their footprints remain. When she fought with another spirit near the Beginning of Time, her bones became a great hill of broken stone. She is Pele, the Hawaiian goddess of the volcano. She is the Spirit of Fire.

The beautiful islands of Hawaii rest like green jade jewels on the bright blue Pacific Ocean. Clear blue skies and white clouds lie above the islands by day. At night, though, it is different. Above the volcano Kilauea, at the mountain Mauna Loa, the clouds turn red like blood because of the fire in Pele's pit-house. This is where Pele lives, but she did not always live there.

Once, near the beginning of time, Pele was just the daughter of Kane-hoa-lane and Haumea. She lived in a grass hut and looked just as human as you or I do. But this was long ago, when many people became great beings with magical powers.

Pele, while she was a pretty young girl, admired

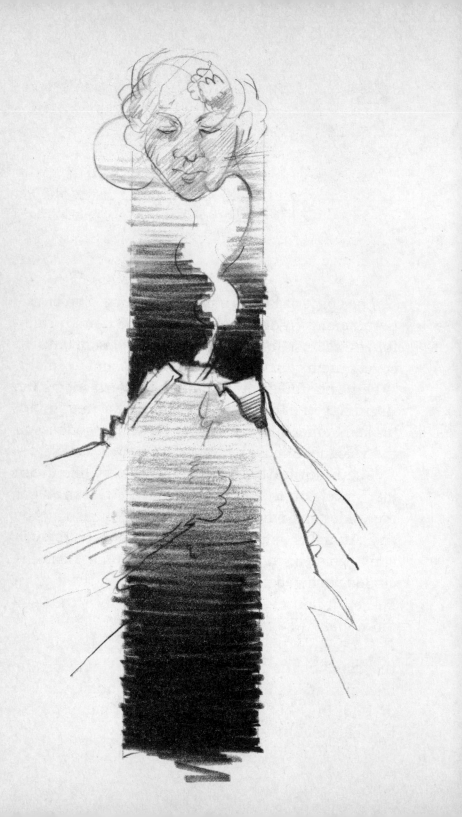

the old Fire God, Lono-Makua. One day she stood so close to him that she herself turned into fire. She accidentally burned down many of the huts and fields, because she was now a fire spirit.

Pele's oldest sister, whose short name was Na-Maka, admired the old Sea God. She stood so near him that she turned into sea water. She flooded many huts and fields by accident, because she was now a sea spirit.

Fire and water will not mix, and these two sisters began to hate one another.

Pele and Na-Maka argued and fought all the time. Because the oldest sister was more powerful, Pele had to run away from home.

Pele and her brothers took the littlest sister Hi'iaka and left in a canoe. They paddled across the rolling sea, looking for a new home. They came to the island of Ni'ihau. It is the island farthest to the north and west in the Hawaiian Island chain. There they all began to dig a pit to live in. Pele wanted a home in the cool earth. She wanted a pit for her and her brothers and sister to live in and show off their ghostly forms as flames or smoke or steam.

As they dug they sang.

> *The flame dances back and forth,*
> *And breaks out above and below.*
> *Our spades make the rocks rattle,*
> *As downward, downward we go.*
> *Who is this digging?*
> *It is Pele digging,*
> *Digging my pit-house on Ni'ihau.*

This song became the very beginning of the hula dance, and the way legends are told in Hawaii.

They dug down deep, but the island was too small. They hit sea water. Fire and water will not mix, so they had to move on.

They went to the south and to the east.

On the island of Kauai, they struck water.

Again, on the island of Oahu, they struck water. Na-Maka, the sea goddess, was chasing them and driving them on.

At Molokai and Lanai the story was the same. Na-Maka would see the glow of Pele's fire at night and would come and send sea water into the pit-house.

On the island of Maui, Pele tried to fight Na-Maka when she came to chase Pele away. They fought and fought, fire against water. Na-Maka even killed Pele and piled her bones into a hill called Bones-of-Pele. Na-Maka poured sea water into the pit-house on Maui.

Pele's brothers and sister moved on without her. They went to the Big Island: Hawaii.

At the Big Island, they looked for a place to dig a pit-house. The ghost of Pele came and floated in the air above the mountain Mauna Loa. "We will dig here," she said.

The brothers and Pele's ghost dug and dug. They did not hit sea water. They dug until they hit the hot lava in the very heart of the Earth itself. Pele had found her home. The volcano Kilauea erupts today as a sign of her presence.

As a ghost, Pele was more powerful than ever.

She ruled over her people. She taught them the hula dance. She chose the man she wanted to be the king of all the Hawaiian Islands. She sent lava against the enemies of that king, and he became the first ruler of all the islands.

Even today, they say Pele does not allow anyone to take rocks off her mountain as souvenirs. Remember that, if you go to Hawaii. Be respectful of the Spirit of Fire!

THE BLOOD SUCKER

When evening fell on the upper Rio Grande River, there was a horrible ghost that floated up and down the river valley. If anyone was walking along the riverbank just at twilight this ghost would come upon them and suck all their blood out!

One day a young Indian woman gave birth to her first child, a girl. The woman and her husband lived in the Indian pueblo of Okeh-Oyngeh. The man had built the house up high to keep it from getting wet if the river flooded. The woman wanted to stay at home for four days for a cleansing ceremony. But the young father wanted to take his baby girl across to the pueblo of Yunkeh-Yunkeh so his mother could see her new granddaughter.

The young mother said, "No! You can't go down in the river valley. It's twilight and the bloodsucker will come!"

The next day the young man was gathering wood and doing his chores. This was the time when the young mother's sisters should come and be with her. His sisters and her sisters would be the ones that would name the infant. He wanted to go into the pueblos to tell the sisters the baby had been born.

But the young mother did not want him to go. They waited four days.

Finally they decided all three would go down to the pueblo for the cleansing ceremony. But the young man's mother was very superstitious and believed the baby should spend each night in the house in which it was born until it had its own name. So, after the cleansing ceremony, the three walked back to their home. They went along the riverbank. The sun was going down. It was becoming twilight.

Just before they were about to cross the footbridge between Okeh-Oyngeh and Yunkeh-Yunkeh, the ghost came whooshing down the river and sucked all the blood out of the mother and the baby. The husband ran to his house and hid, filled with anger and grief.

He asked the good spirits to give him strength, and he rubbed holy corn meal on his face. Finally he knew what to do. He spent all the next day making sharp spears. Then he followed the path of blood on the grass until he found the cave where the bloodsucker hid in the heat of the day.

He took all the spears and stuck them in the ground around the mouth of the cave. He stuck them in with their sharp points pointed inward.

He went down by the riverbank at twilight and called out in a loud voice. The ghost heard him and came whooshing out of its cave to get him. As it rushed out it hit sharp spears on all sides. The spears cut the ghost into thousands of little pieces.

The blood on the grasses turned into Indian paintbrush with its blood-red flower.

The thousands of pieces of the bloodsucker became mosquitoes.

So now if you go down to the Rio Grande between Okeh-Oyngeh and Yunkeh-Yunkeh, there are mosquitoes there.

And they will suck the blood right out of you!

Jack and the
Sally-Bally

Once upon a time in the wooded hills of the Ozarks, there lived a smart young boy named Jack. He had climbed a bean plant, and he had killed a giant, but now he was visiting his grandma and grandpa in their log cabin in a valley.

Up in the hills above Jack's grandma's cabin, there lived a monster that folks called the Sally-Bally. He would come sallying forth into the valley and scare the people. He would eat their horses and cows and kick down their log cabins just for meanness. The Sally-Bally was one bad critter. Sometimes he even ate people!

It was autumn when Jack came for his visit. Jack's grandpa had a crop of apples in his orchard that were the biggest, reddest, sweetest apples Jack had ever seen. The smell of those apples cooking in a big black pot over an outdoor fire filled the valley.

All the neighbors smelled the apples when they were cooking.

So did the Sally-Bally.

That old Sally-Bally had come down out of the hills two times before, picked up the big black pot hot from the fire, and drunk the apples like a jug of cider. He would have eaten Jack's grandma and grandpa, too, if they hadn't run away and hid for two days.

Jack's grandpa needed to pick more apples to take to town and sell for some cash-money. Jack agreed to help him. They took two big buckets and went into the orchard to pick. The apples were so good that they ate a few while they were picking. The smell of those sweet, sweet apples filled the air and woke the sleeping Sally-Bally in his cave.

"You know," said Grandpa, "We ought to make a Sally-Bally trap and use these apples as bait." Soon they were both bragging about how easily they could catch that old Sally-Bally. They began to laugh and joke about it and forgot to keep watch for the Sally-Bally.

Sure enough, over the hill came the Sally-Bally, brought by the smell of the apples. The Sally-Bally was twenty feet tall, with eighteen feet of him legs. He had long, ugly hair and ears as big as the bed of a wagon. His arms hung so low they dragged the ground, and his mouth had so many teeth it looked like a laundry basket full of butcher knives!

The Sally-Bally roared like a mountain lion arguing with a steam engine. Jack and his grandpa began to run toward the house with the Sally-Bally chasing them. Jack threw down his bucket of apples, and the critter stopped to eat them—bucket and all. When the Sally-Bally had almost caught up to Jack and his grandpa, Grandpa threw down his bucket, and the critter stopped to eat those apples, too.

While the Sally-Bally was picking his teeth with

the bail of the second bucket, Jack and Grandpa ran to the cabin and yelled for Grandma to run and hide.

"Run, Grandma," yelled Jack. "Here comes the Sally-Bally!"

Knowing they didn't have enough time to run away, Jack and Grandpa turned over the big black pot in the front yard and hid under it.

Grandma was sitting on the front porch taking in the cool breeze and weaving on her wooden loom. She saw Jack and his grandpa come running. She even saw the Sally-Bally come over the hill and look around for them after they had hidden under the big black pot. But Grandma was a tough old lady, and she just puffed on her pipe and went on weaving on her loom.

The Sally-Bally came dragging over to the cabin, stepped over the black pot without looking under it, and growled at Grandma. "Where are those men-folks at?" growled the Sally-Bally.

"I ain't seen them," said Grandma, weaving on her loom.

"You'd better tell me where they're at," said the Sally-Bally, leaning over the roof of the porch and blowing his hot stinky breath down on Grandma, "or I'll smash your porch flat!"

The porch was Grandma's most favorite place to be,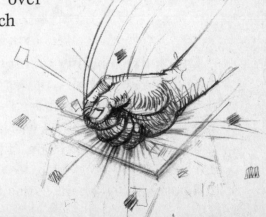

so that threat made her mad. "Lean over here close
if you want to hear," she said to the Sally-Bally. He
leaned way down and put his big old ear to the
porch.

Quick like a bunny rabbit Grandma jumped into
the Sally-Bally's hairy old ear and pulled her loom
and rocking chair in after her. Then she sat back
down and went back to work, rocking in her chair
and weaving on her loom. The noise almost drove
the Sally-Bally crazy!

The rocking chair squeaked and the weaving

loom creaked. The Sally-Bally jumped around in circles, hollering and yelling. He scratched his ear and he shook his head and he rolled on the ground. But Grandma was used to riding in a wagon over the roads in the Ozarks, and this ride in the critter's ear was mild by comparison.

Finally the Sally-Bally couldn't stand the noise of the rocking chair and the weaving loom any longer. He decided to beat his head against a nearby cliff to see if he couldn't knock the grandma and her furniture out of his ear. He stood beside the cliff and beat his big ugly head on the rock so hard that he fell down dead.

By now Jack and his Grandpa had come out from under the black pot and had run up to help Grandma. They carried the loom between them and Grandma carried the rocking chair upside down on her head. The three walked back to the cabin in the valley and cooked a big pot of apples.

"Well," said Jack to his grandma, "Now that you've killed the Sally-Bally what are you going to do with him?"

"Ain't going to do nothing," said Grandma. "The moss will grow on him, and the ferns will grow on him, and the weeds will grow on him, and by next spring you won't even know he was ever there."

And, you know, she was right!

AFTERWORD
for parents, teachers, and librarians

All children love stories: they love to hear them told, to hear them read aloud, and eventually, to read and tell them for themselves. Stories are a vital part of a child's learning and emotional growth. They help children expand their view of the world. They help them work through the emotional stresses of childhood (such as the conflict between wanting, on the one hand, to be coddled by mother, and on the other, to go forth into the world outside the family). Stories help children face fear and master it. It is in this last way that scary stories are helpful, not harmful, to children.

The earliest teaching was done in the form of story-telling, from tribal stories around the campfire, to the *exempla* of the Roman academies, to the parables of Jesus. In many European languages, *story* and *history* are the same word, and both serve the same purpose of teaching and preparing young minds for future accomplishments. As the school curriculum has grown more complex and the sheer quantities of information to be taught have increased, storytelling has been relegated more to the pre-school years and early primary school grades.

Although stories and storytelling are an important part of adult life in many regions of the world, and should so remain, many Americans think of stories as a childhood pursuit. This comes from the emotional response most adults have to three types of stories: fantasy is widely regarded as juvenile, historical fiction as more mature, and true history or adult fiction (which confines itself to "believable" characters and settings) as the most mature—and therefore suited to the most mature reading audience. This creates a false separation between stories read silently by an adult and stories read or told aloud to children.

Many adults assume that if a story is to be told aloud, it must be because the listeners are unable to read it for themselves—thus the listeners must be children, and the story one suited only for a juvenile audience. The fact that many stories in the oral tradition (told aloud from teller to listener, and passed on without being written down) are fantasy reinforces the supposed distinction between "stories told to kids" and "books read by adults."

Throughout the world where traditions are honored, and in all pre-literate societies, fantasy stories are told, heard, and enjoyed by audiences of all ages—as is also the case in many parts of America where older traditions are maintained, such as in the Appalachians and the Ozarks. The stories in this book, too, are just as likely to be told by adults to other adults around a campfire as they are to be read aloud to children around a candle on Hallowe'en night.

Most of us who listen to stories love fantasy, but not nearly so much as children do. Children throughout the world adore fantasy for several reasons.

- Young children, just beginning to think and speak their own thoughts, assume that animals and toys must also have these thoughts and things to say. Stories about talking animals and inanimate objects that come to life are of great appeal to them.

- Children also constantly use their imaginations to embellish their daily lives, and the extraordinary details of a typical fantasy story provide them new material for personal fantasizing.

- Fantasy stories for children—unlike those written for adult readers—almost always portray the elements of conflict in clear, good-versus-evil terms, with good triumphant in the end. This appeals to the strong moral sense of children, and tends to reinforce the moral teaching of their adult caregivers.

Most appealing of all to children, though, is the way fantasy stories establish the conflict necessary to *any* good story in simple terms they can understand.

Children don't fear the same things grown-ups do. A story for us might threaten its central character with failure, rejection, impotency, or loss of wealth or status. The heroes of children's fantasy tales are threatened with simpler things: being eaten by a troll, for example, or being cooked in an oven by a witch. Children understand these simple dangers and experience fear for the safety of the heroes and then both relief and mastery of former fear when the heroes triumph in the end. When the witch is cooked in her own oven or the troll overeats and explodes, the story teaches that the evildoer is undone by his, her, or *its* own evil ways: evil gets punished.

Because of the vicarious fear and triumph children experience in frightening fantasies (a powerful thrill too many of us bigger people have forgotten in the years since childhood), scary stories are often their favorites. This both puzzles and disturbs adults. For the conflict in fantasies to be simple enough for children to understand, the threat must be simple, and often gruesome and grotesque—the threat of being eaten by a tiger who crunches on people's bones, for example. Parents, teachers, and librarians are sometimes concerned that the violence and gore (present or implied) in scary stories will be bad for children. This is not so.

Even the goriest fairy tales provide hope through happy endings. The most violent of them offer the child both positive and negative examples of behavior: a child wants to be like Yurr, the smart sister in "The Tiger's Eyes," not like the foolish wife whose punishment for inattention is to be eaten by the tiger. In spite of the dangers of the tiger in man's clothing, Yurr uses her skill at observation and her intelligence to outwit the tiger; she relies on her extended family; she offers care to the small birds who help rescue her; she tries in vain to save the foolish members of the tiger's "family." In short, she is both a perfect heroine and a strong incentive to listeners to be more like her. The ghastly crunch of the devoured victims' bones is forgotten in the triumphant outcome.

Without the threat of the tiger, there would be no conflict. Without the conflict, there would be no storyline. Without the storyline, there would be no triumphant outcome, no behavioral model, and no learning or personal growth for the listener.

Of course children can be scarred by violence—in war zones or in the streets of some inner cities, by domestic violence and abuse, perhaps even by entertainment media with their portrayals of violence. The violence in fairy tales is different:

... the storyteller or reader is *present* to give moral support to the child audience

... the fear is centered on the storyline and is mastered as the story reaches its conclusion with hero and audience intact (true even when the child is old enough to read the story alone in his or her room), and

... the "distance" between the real world and the events of the story is great enough that the child returns to his or her own real world without the fear felt while "inside" the story.

Because scary stories, like all fairy tales, both instruct and entertain, Lewis Carroll called them "a love-gift" *(Through the Looking Glass)*. Wilhelm Grimm, referring to the powerful psychological messages in them, said "fairy tales are tiny jewels of belief fragments whose significance is lost but still felt." Johann Schiller wrote, "Deeper meaning abides in the fairy tales told to me in my childhood than in the truth that is taught by life" *(Die Piccolomini, Act III, Scene 4)*. For G.K. Chesterton, "the things I believed most in [the nursery], the things I believe most now, are the things called fairy tales." "My first and last philosophy," he said, "...I learnt in the nursery" *(Orthodoxy)*.

Each of these men—writers, poet, philosopher—presents the same message: fairy tales, fantasy stories, scary tales with their imaginary violence, all teach moral principles, good social behavior, courage, heroism, and hope.

Two more recent works address the specific issue of violence in fantasy stories, fairy tales, and scary stories. Ephraim Biblow's article "Imaginative Play and the Control of Aggressive Behavior," in Jerome Singer's *The*

Child's World of Make-Believe (New York: Academic Press, 1973) shows evidence that a rich fantasy life allows a child to deal with aggression inside that fantasy life rather than outside in the real world. Bruno Bettelheim, in his *The Uses of Enchantment: The Meaning and Importance of Fairy Tales* (New York: Vantage Books, 1989) shows that "the original displeasure of anxiety" or fear for the fate of the story's central characters "turns into the great pleasure of anxiety successfully faced and mastered."

The conscientious parent, teacher, or librarian will always need to know a great deal about the story-listening audience, and must make some choices about the age-appropriateness of scary stories for each audience. Even so, the adult reviewer should not arbitrarily reject a story based on its potentially fearful content.

In general, children are a better judge of what frightens them than adults are. The story teller or reader should always watch the reactions of the audience to the story. A fearful facial expression is normal as the child works through the anxiety and masters it. If a story becomes too scary for a small child, he will seek a lap to sit in, or cover his ears, or ask you to stop.

In the rare event that a story is too scary for a child, the storyteller or reader should stop briefly and help the child master the fear. Explain, for example, that trolls don't live in your city (but not that trolls don't exist— that insults the child's fear). Or, you may paraphrase the rest of the story and move quickly to the happy ending. Don't simply stop the story: the ending is necessary to master the fear and instill hope. Usually, when a child is frightened and does not want to hear the end of a story, he will ask to hear that story again months or years later, when he is ready to face and master his fear of it.

The stories in this book have been carefully selected through years of retelling, and are all identified by children from across the nation as being among their favorites. Each story has a symbol indicating the proper age range for its audience. All the stories can be read by ten-year-olds with an average vocabulary, although they will not enjoy the stories for five- to six- year-olds as much. When regional words (e.g., catalpa tree) are used, some explanation might be necessary by the storyteller. When regional names are used (e.g., Ni'ihau) and considered important to the story, they are explained in the Guide to Pronunciation.

Acknowledgments

The editors wish to thank the many people who have assisted us in the preparation of this collection of scary stories. For research assistance, we thank Benjamin Corey Miller, Mary Roberts Bishop, Ronnie and Terry Brown, and Stephanie Dugan. For library research into the origins and variations of these stories, we wish to thank Janet Watkins, Dennis VanArsdale, and Lucille Pratt. Our special appreciation goes to Martha Ledbetter and storytellers Marilyn Kinsella and Margaret Miller Anderson for help in the gathering of children's responses to these stories.

Among the children, many of whose names we never learned, we wish to thank the children of our friends, especially Nicole, Claire, Lydia, Steve, Lacey, Brian, Honey, and Isaac. To our families, friends, and all the folks at August House who helped, we extend our heartfelt thanks.

Richard and Judy Dockrey Young

Original Collection Notes

BLOOD-RED CEDAR is an Ozark variant/fragment of Grimm's "The Juniper Tree." An even shorter fragment, collected by folklorist Vance Randolph in Missouri in the 1930's, is told as "Pennywinkle! Pennywinkle!" Our version is based on fragments collected from adults who remembered the story from childhood.

THE BLOODSUCKER is a Pueblo Indian story from northern New Mexico loved by children. This version was collected in 1989 from Teresa Pijoan de Van Etten, nationally-known storyteller. If there is any error in our telling, it is ours, and not that of Mrs. Van Etten.

BLOODY MARY, BLOODY MARY has nation-wide popularity as a story and as a playful childhood "experiment" in ghost hunting. Three different children provided us with versions of it in a scary story session at a campground in 1989.

THE CHANGELINGS is a fragment/variant of a Norwegian folktale. Our variant was collected in part in Fergus Falls, Minnesota, in 1963, when girls from different states gathered at the home of Barb Putnam and told stories. Hank and Becky Hartman of LaCrosse,

Wisconsin assisted in research into the story at Westerheim Museum in Decorah, Iowa, in 1986.

THE GHOST OF VENGEANCE is the most famous Japanese ghost story, brought to America after World War II and told among Japanese-American children ever since. We are indebted to Yoichi Aoki in 1973, Marilyn Aoki in 1987, and Suzette Raney in 1990 for assistance in preparing our version of the story.

THE GOLEM is a recent fragment/variant of "The Golem of Prague," a favorite story among Jewish children in many nations. This story was first collected in part from Phillip Freid at age nine.

THE HOBBYAHS, also published as "The Hobyahs," was first anthologized in 1894. A favorite among English and American children, our version was collected from Donna Lakin in 1985. This story is in the public domain.

THE KI'IN SPIRITS is a favorite children's story among the K'mu refugees from Cambodia. We are indebted to Doug Lipman, storyteller, Medford, Massachusetts (1983), and Sadiah Jantan (1990) for K'mu and Indonesian versions of this story.

MARRIED TO A GHOST is one variant of the stories known by the Chinook Indian tribe of the Pacific Northwest as "Chinook Ghosts" or "Blue Jay and Ioi," and by the Klickitat tribe as "The Memaloose Islands." It is a children's favorite in Washington and Oregon. We heard one version at the National Storytelling Festival in 1983.

OLD RAW HEAD, also called "Bloody Bones and Rawhide," is the favorite children's story in the Arkansas Ozarks. Hundreds of children have told us versions of the story since 1968. We are also indebted to JoAnne Sears Rife (1975), Teresa Pijoan de Van Etten (1988), and Virginia Kirby Nickels (1990) for their contributions to this version.

RAGGELUGG is an English children's story first anthologized in the 1880's. Becky Fraley heard this version in childhood and first provided it to us in 1978. This story is in the public domain.

RAP...RAP...RAP! is a favorite children's nonsense story that introduces them to the concept of the pun. Alice White first told this story to Judy in childhood.

THE RED VELVET RIBBON is called "The Red Thread" in Europe, and was first anthologized by Washington Irving. Two ten-year-olds outshouted each other to tell this version to us in 1989.

JACK AND THE SALLY-BALLY is a variant of a Midwestern folktale that Vance Randolph collected as "Sally Bally Cato." This version was provided by children from Arkansas, Missouri, Kansas, and Oklahoma between 1981 and 1990.

SHE'S GOT ME! is a folktale and urban legend throughout the English-speaking world. We have heard variants from teens and pre-teens from many states; one even said it actually happened to his father, but it was a Scout knife through the cuff of his trousers that pinned him to the grave. Tom Phillips of Edmond, Oklahoma, gave us this version in 1977.

SKUNNEE WUNDEE (or SKUNNY-WUNDY) AND THE STONE GIANT is a favorite children's story in the Northeast. Of Algonkian Indian origin, our version is based on the tellings of Joe Bruchac, a New York State Abenaki Indian, and on versions learned from children.

SPIRIT OF FIRE is a fragment of the complex Pele legend, which exists in four distinct versions in Hawaii. Keli'i Kalemanu of Honolulu provided us with this material in 1988. The Pele stories are sacred to the Native Hawaiians, and any error in the telling is ours, not that of Mr. Kalemanu.

STOP THE COFFIN! is a nonsense punning story, often referring to Smith Brothers (TM) Cough Drops. Dr. Morgan M. Young, Ed.D., (1902–1982) and Lewin Hayden Dockrey (1920–1989) told their children variants, making this the only story common to both childhoods of the editors of this collection.

THE TIGER'S EYES is a children's favorite among the refugees of the Hmong people of Laos, brought to America after 1972. This version was provided to us in 1989 by May Yang.

WHAM! SLAM! JENNY-MO-JAM! is known and has been published under many names. A children's favorite in the Old South, this variant was collected by Texas folklorist Peggy Shamburger Hendricks from her great-aunt Betty Shamburger Atwood, who had in turn learned it from Aunt Hattie, the family's nurse and cook, in about 1900. Children ask for or tell us this story under many names, including "Barney McCabe..." and "Wylie and His Sister."

THE WHITE WOLF is one of hundreds of similar stories of animal albinism and human/animal spiritualism. Although there is a Fort Phantom Hill in Texas, there is no historical connection between the name and this story, which was first told to us by Otis Johnson at age eleven.

WHO'S FOLLOWING ME? has been told to us by children for forty years. This version was first told to us by Phillip Squires at age eleven.

WYLIE AND THE HAIRY MAN is known throughout the Appalachians and the Southeast by many names in hundreds of variations. It is the most-often heard and requested story among children in those regions. We are indebted to Margaret Miller Anderson, storyteller at King's Mountain State Park, South Carolina, for this variant.

A Guide to Pronunciation

Many of the stories have words or names that are not in English, because America is home to so many different kinds of people. In this guide to help you pronounce the words, we have used the sounds of English words whenever possible. When no English sound is easily found, follow this pattern:

ah, like the sound of the "a" in father
eh, like the sound of the "e" in best
ee, like the sound of the "ee" in seen
oh, like the sound of the letter "o" in go
oo, like the sound of the "oo" in food
ih, like the sound of the letter "i" in pin

golem: The first syllable is like the English word "go." The second syllable is like the first half of the word "lemon." *(GOH-lehm)*

A being made from clay or stone and brought to life by magic.

Gunze: Using the sound patterns above, say *GOON-zeh.*

One of Otto-san's friends.

Haumea: Using the sound patterns above, say *HAH-oo-MEH-ah.*

One of the ancient goddesses of the South Pacific, mother of Pele.

Hi'iaka: Using the sound patterns above, say *HEE-ee-AH-kah.*
> Pele's younger sister, so small that she was hidden in an empty bird egg for the long canoe journey across the Pacific toward Hawaii. Pele carried Hi'iaka under her arm.

Hobbyahs: Sometimes spelled "Hobyahs." Just say the word "hobby," then say "ahs." *(HAHB-yahz)*
> Monsters that eat people in an old English folktale.

Kaminasu: Using the sound patterns above, say *kah-mee-NAH-soo.*
> He is one of Otto-san's friends.

Kane-hoa-lane: Using the sound patterns above, say *KAH-neh-HOH-ah-LAH-neh.*
> One of the ancient gods of the South Pacific, father of Pele.

Kauai: Say what a crow says: "caw." Then say the word "eye." *(KAH-oo-ah-ee)*
> One of the islands of Hawaii.

Ki'in: The first sound is the same as the word "kit" without the *t*, and the second sound rhymes with "mean." *(Kih-EEN)*
> In the K'mu or Kammu language of Cambodia, a word sounding like this is the name of evil cannibal spirits.

Kilauea: Say the word *kee-lah-WEH-ah.*
> The famous volcano in Hawaii.

Lanai: Say the word *LAH-nah-ee.*
> One of the islands of Hawaii.

Lono-Makua: Say the word *LOH-noh-MAHK-oo-ah.*
The ancient fire god of the South Pacific.

Matsue: Say it *maht-SOO-weh.*
The warrior's young lover in "The Ghost of
Vengeance."

Maui: The first part rhymes with "now," and the
second part is "ee" on the list of patterns above.
(MAH-oo-ee)
One of the islands of Hawaii.

Mauna Loa: Say it *MAH-oo-nah-LOH-ah.*
The mountain on which Kilauea Volcano sits.

Molokai: Say it *MOH-loh-kah-ee.*
One of the islands of Hawaii.

Na-Maka: Say it *Nah-MAH-kah.*
Pele's older sister and a sea goddess.

Ni'ihau: Say the word "knee", then say "ee" and the
word "how." *(Nee-EE-hah-oo)*
One of the islands of Hawaii.

Oahu: Say "Oh," then say the cheer "Wahoo!"
(Oh-WAH-hoo)
One of the islands of Hawaii, where the capital
Honolulu is located.

Oiwa: The first syllable rhymes with "boy," the
second sounds like "wand" without the last two
letters. *(OY-wah)*
The lady who is murdered and becomes the
Ghost of Vengeance.

Okeh-Oyngeh: Also spelled Oke-Oyuinge. Say it
OH-keh-oh-EEN-geh.
An ancient Pueblo Indian village no longer
inhabited in New Mexico.

Otto-san: Say it *Oh-toh-sahn.*
> In one dialect of Japanese it means "honorable husband." In other dialects *oto-san* means "father" and *shujin* means "husband." He is the evil warrior in "The Ghost of Vengeance."

Pele: The first sound is like "pet" without the *t*, and the second sound is like "let" without the *t (PEH-leh)*
> She is the Hawaiian goddess of fire.

Raggelugg: The first two syllables sound like "raggy" and the last one sounds like "lug."
> In the old Anglo-Saxon language, *ragge* meant a fluff of fur and *luggen* meant to pull by the ear. So Raggelugg's name tells what happened to him in the story, which comes from England originally.

samurai: The first syllable sounds like the first syllable of the word "somber." The second syllable is just "oo" from the list of sounds. The last syllable sounds like the English word "rye." *(SAH-moo-rye)*
> A Japanese warrior.

Skunnee Wundee: Sometimes spelled "Skunny-Wundy." Both syllables rhyme with the word "sunny." *(SKUH-nee WUHN-dee)*
> An Indian boy who is kin to the animals and the hero of many scary and amusing stories among the Algonkian-speaking people.

Yotsuya: Use the patterns above to pronounce the word *yoht-SOO-yah.*
> A district in Japan where the story of Oiwa takes place. "The Ghost of Vengeance" is also called "Yotsuya Kaidan or "The Tale of the Ghost from Yotsuya."

Yunkeh-Yunkeh: Also spelled "Yunke-Yunke."
Say it *YOON-keh-YOON-keh.*

An ancient Pueblo Indian village in New Mexico where no one lives anymore.

Yurr: Rhymes with "sir."

Yurr (also spelled *yer*) is the Hmong word for "little sister" in Laos.

MORE SCARY STORIES FROM
Richard & Judy Dockrey Young

**Favorite Scary Stories of
American Children**
Audiobook (grades K–3) $12.00 /
ISBN 0-87483-148-2
Audiobook (grades 4–6) $12.00 /
ISBN 0-87483-175-X

Ozark Ghost Stories
Paperback $12.95 / ISBN 0-87483-410-4
Audiobook $12.00 / ISBN 0-87483-211-X

The Scary Story Reader
Paperback $11.95 / ISBN 0-87483-382-5
Hardback $19.00 / ISBN 0-87483-271-3

**Ghost Stories from the
American Southwest**
Paperback $9.95
ISBN 0-87483-174-1
Audiobook $12.00 / ISBN 0-87483-149-0

**There's No Such
Thing as Ghosts**
Ghost Stories from the Southeast
Audiobook $12.00 / ISBN 0-87483-333-7

The Head on the High Road
Ghost Stories from the Southwest
Audiobook $12.00 / ISBN 0-87483-334-5

MORE SCARY STORIES FROM
August House Publishers

**Queen of the
Cold-Blooded Tales**
ROBERTA SIMPSON BROWN
Paperback $9.95 / ISBN 0-87483-408-2
Hardback $19.95 / ISBN 0-87483-332-9

Tales of an October Moon
MARC JOEL LEVITT
Audiobook $12.00 / ISBN 0-87483-209-8

Cajun Ghost Stories
J.J. RENEAUX
Audiobook $12.00 / ISBN 0-87483-210-1

Scared in School
ROBERTA SIMPSON BROWN
Paperback $8.95 / ISBN 0-87483-496-1

The Tell-Tale Heart
& Other Terrifying Tales
SYD LIEBERMAN
Audiobook $12.00 / ISBN 0-87483-430-9

The Scariest Stories Ever
ROBERTA SIMPSON BROWN
Audiobook $12.00 / ISBN 0-87483-301-9

Animal Ghost Stories
NANCY ROBERTS
Hardback $14.95 / ISBN 0-87483-401-5

Ghostwise
A Book of Midnight Stories
DAN YASHINSKY
Paperback $11.95 / ISBN 0-87483-499-6